CW01498341

WHOEVER FIGHTS MONSTERS

By

Angelo Marcos

WHOEVER FIGHTS MONSTERS

About the Author

Angelo Marcos is a writer, comedian and actor, and a graduate of both law and psychology.

He has performed stand-up comedy all over the UK, and has acted in numerous short films and theatrical productions.

He co-wrote the musical 'Love and Marriage' which was performed at the Edinburgh Festival, and also contributed to the Royal British Legion book 'In the Footsteps of War'.

His articles and short stories have been published both online and in print, and his novels and short story collections are available in both ebook and paperback formats.

Find out more and get a free copy of short story Killing Time at **www.angelomarcos.com**

For my son, Anthony.

I love you and I'm proud of you.
And that will always be true.

"Whoever fights monsters should see to it that in the process he does not become a monster."

Friedrich Nietzsche, ***Beyond Good and Evil***
(aphorism 146)

Chapter 1

"You'll be great, princess," Nathaniel said into the phone. "Just relax."

"But what if I mess up the middle part, Dad?"

"You won't," he said kindly, remembering the thousand mornings he'd been rudely awakened by the sound of piano keys being massacred.

Before the separation, obviously.

"Have you been practising every day like I said?"

"Kind of…"

"Then it'll be fine, princess."

He opened his desk drawer and looked nervously at the gun. He'd already loaded it and fitted the suppressor. Everything was ready.

He glanced at his watch. Nearly time. His breath caught in his throat.

Could he really do this?

"Dad?!"

"Yes?"

"I said, do you promise?"

"Do I..? Yes! Of course. I promise, princess. It'll be great. *You'll* be great."

1

He shut the drawer and leaned forward in an attempt to stop his legs from shaking. It didn't work.

"OK, Dad. If you say so."

"Everything will turn out OK. Remember, nothing worth having ever came without a struggle. And remember, everybody loves Miss Amanda. And why does everybody love you?"

"Dad…"

"No, come on. Why does everybody love my beautiful Princess Amanda?"

"Because I'm lovely," she said in her best humouring-my-dad voice. She was way off being a teenager, but had that particular tone of voice down pat.

"Exactly. And don't you forget it."

"See you tomorrow, Dad."

"See you tomorrow, princess. I love you."

"I love you too, Dad."

He placed the phone back in its cradle, noting what a struggle it was with his hand trembling. He stared at the door. William was due any minute now, he had to be ready.

Aurora sat patiently in the corner of the room. Nathaniel caught her gaze and she smiled, her face telling him everything he needed to know. He could do this. He needed to.

It was the only way to save his daughter.

Chapter 2

Two minutes later, there was a knock at the door.

"Come in," Nathaniel said, swallowing down the nausea that threatened to bubble up at any moment. His clothes suddenly felt too tight, and he undid the top button of his shirt.

The question he had asked himself earlier recurred.

Could he really do this?

Of course he could. After all, what choice did he have?

William Kwang walked into the office, the overpowering scent of his aftershave almost arriving first. He was a fairly big man, although Nathaniel was never clear how much of that was fat and how much was muscle.

"You wanted to see me boss?"

"Yes, please sit down, Will."

The younger man lowered himself into the seat in front of Nathaniel's desk and leaned slightly to the left, inadvertently putting himself directly opposite the gun barrel in the drawer.

Nathaniel could do it now. He could open the drawer, take the gun, and just do it now. He looked over at Aurora, who shook her head.

The message was clear. Not yet.

"Will," Nathaniel started, "would you be able to work a little late tonight? Something's come up."

He gave a theatrical sigh.

"How long do you need me?" he asked.

"Well, that's the thing, we might not get finished until around midnight."

William looked up at the clock on the wall behind Nathaniel, drawing out the action for maximum effect.

"That's another six hours, boss," he said. "I'm not sure…"

"There'll be overtime pay of course," Nathaniel said. "Time and a half until eight, and then double after that."

William's face broke into a broad grin.

"That's all you had to say, boss."

Nathaniel tried to smile but the nerves wouldn't allow him to. His palms felt wet, and he was sure his forehead would be drenched too. His eyes stung slightly, probably as sweat from his brow poured into his eyes.

This was madness. Nathaniel Bennett wasn't a killer. What was he *doing*? He felt a sudden desire to bolt, to get out of the room and never look back.

One thing stopped him. This was the only way to save Amanda.

And he could do this for her. He knew he could do anything for her.

"D-Do you need to call anyone?" he asked.

"My girl. She'll be worried otherwise," William said, standing up and heading to the door.

"No, no," Nathaniel blurted to his confused looking employee. "Call from here."

"Are you sure?"

"Of course," Nathaniel said, trying to keep his voice even and his face relaxed.

William sat back down.

"Here," Nathaniel said, passing his desk phone to William and looking over at Aurora for some kind of guidance.

William dialled, every so often glancing up at his boss as though this were some trick. He turned his head as if trying to see who Nathaniel was looking at.

"I'm very tired, Will," he said quickly. "Once we get everything done tonight, I'll feel better. We've got a lot of work to do, that's all."

His breathing was shallow and rapid. He hoped William hadn't noticed.

William nodded, seemingly placated, and told whoever answered the phone that he wouldn't be back until the morning. As he did, Nathaniel retrieved the gun from his drawer, holding it low so that William wouldn't see.

The younger man hung up the phone and looked over at Nathaniel.

"So what now, boss?"

Nathaniel looked over at Aurora, who gave a solemn nod.

He felt his body inexplicably relax and took a long, deep breath as if bracing himself for impact.

An image flashed into his mind. William Kwang standing in front of a school as it exploded, killing Nathaniel's little girl and all her classmates.

He stood, aimed the gun at William, and fired three shots.

The last two were unnecessary. The first one – a head shot – killed him instantly.

Chapter 3

There was so much blood.

Nathaniel had never seen a dead body before, let alone one that he himself had caused to die. He suddenly felt as if he would be sick.

Aurora was at his side in an instant.

"Put the gun on the desk, Nathaniel," she said in the soothing tone he'd become so familiar with. "All you have to do is put the gun on your desk. That's all you have to do. Everything is OK."

He looked at her and her gaze acted like an anchor to his listing ship. As if by looking at her, the raging storm had let up, and the sun had broken through the dark clouds. Her eyes calmed him, they had done since the first time he'd met her.

He slowly sat back down and put the gun on the desk. Blood pulsed out of the slumped body of his employee in a sick rhythm, as though the wound itself was vomiting the life out of him.

He stared – unable to look away – until the pulsing abruptly stopped. William Kwang no longer existed, he was just a body now. A shell of rapidly-cooling flesh and bone.

"His heart," Aurora explained, as if reading his thoughts. "It's stopped now. No more pumping, no more blood. It's OK, Nathaniel. It's done now. You're saving a lot of people from a lot of pain. You're saving the lives of children."

He didn't feel like he was saving anybody. And staring at the slumped, lifeless body of his former employee only strengthened that view. His stomach lurched and he swallowed down the rising bile, clenching every muscle in his body so as to not to be sick. He closed his eyes – looking at a corpse was not helping.

It's not William, it's a body. Just a shell.

"So… what do I do now?" he asked his guide in this waking nightmare.

"We just follow the plan, Nathaniel. Put him in the unit, then we go to the hotel."

He nodded slowly. The nausea was passing, although he didn't know when it would rise up again so wanted to seize the moment.

"Nathaniel, remember that you know what these men planned to do. You've seen it. You've experienced it. You're saving a lot of people. You're saving Amanda."

He both flinched and felt emboldened at the use of his daughter's name. He was doing this for her, of course he was. His job was to protect his family. He was a good dad, after all.

"That's right," Aurora said, "you are protecting them Nathaniel."

He looked back at the body – no longer seeing it as an employee at the office supply company in which they worked, but as the murderer he knew it would've become had he let it live.

Nathaniel took off his blazer, rolled up his sleeves, and walked over to the free-standing cupboard on the wall of his office. He'd emptied it earlier – at Aurora's request, of course – so he knew William would fit inside.

No, not William. Not anymore. Just a shell. Just a body.

He opened the door, then walked over to *the body*, hoisted it up and sat it down in the base of the cupboard.

He looked away as he carried it, trying not to focus on the wet, bloody bullet hole in the top of the head. As he folded its arms across its chest, Nathaniel heard a moan from the body and jumped back. His heartbeat suddenly ratcheted up as visions of the body somehow fighting back danced into his head. He knew it was impossible, but as he well knew, emotion always trumped intellect.

"It's OK," he heard Aurora say, "he's dead, Nathaniel. You compressed his chest and some air came out of his lungs, that's all."

Nathaniel stared at the body, watching for any slight movement, any further noise, anything that might suggest that the corpse was somehow no longer dead. There was nothing.

"Nathaniel," Aurora said gently.

He stared at the two bullet holes in the top of the body's head and the one in its forehead. His mind flashed back to moments ago – which was a lifetime ago now. The first bullet he fired entered the forehead, and as the head slumped forward the next two bullets entered the skull mere inches apart. It was, in short, a mess.

"Nathaniel."

He'd crossed a line now. No going back. His mission had well and truly begun.

"Nathaniel," she said with a sense of urgency, "we have six hours until he's missed, maybe longer if his girlfriend falls asleep and doesn't miss him until the morning. But we can't take that risk. Lock the cupboard door, Nathaniel, then we have to leave."

She was right, of course she was. If there's one thing Nathaniel had learned it was that Aurora was always right.

All at once he heard the vague, distant sound of children's screams echoing around his head. He recognised the cacophony, and knew it would only build and grow louder and more horrific if he didn't act. He looked at Aurora.

"Please, don't," he said.

"I'm just reminding you what will happen, Nathaniel. We need to move quickly so we can stop the others. If we don't, they will die, Nathaniel. You have to save them."

"I will," he said, a renewed determination flowing through his veins. "I will."

He pushed the body's foot into the cupboard, then closed and locked the door. It wasn't a heavy lock, it was the type used to protect confidential files in an office so probably wouldn't withstand much of an effort to break in, but it would keep the door closed for long enough. He didn't understand exactly how the plan was going to work, but Aurora had told him what to do and assured him that as long as he followed her lead, he'd be OK.

He walked over to his desk and retrieved the gun. He'd never shot a gun before and was surprised at how quiet it had been. Under Aurora's instruction, he'd bought it from someone on the dark web, half-expecting it to not work. He'd been told it was the same type of gun that the Navy

Seals used on covert missions, and that the suppressor coupled with the type of bullets – subsonic, apparently – would make the shots as quiet as possible. There was no such thing as a silent gunshot, but there were ways to muffle the sound by using a suppressor. Coupled with ammunition that when fired wouldn't break the sound barrier and cause a sonic boom, it'd be quiet enough. The equipment had definitely done the job.

He looked over at the cupboard where the crumpled body was probably rapidly cooling. Aurora had told him that rigor mortis doesn't set in immediately, but can start at around four hours after death which was still pretty quick.

He thought about the body stuck in that awkward position, like a screwed up and discarded piece of paper. Then he thought about the victims Aurora had shown him, the children that *the body* and his friends would have gone on to target in a bombing campaign which would be described by the media as 'the embodiment of evil itself'. One or two of the children had looked crumpled in death too – charred and twisted. They wouldn't be now though. Nathaniel was saving them.

"We have to go, Nathaniel," Aurora said. "We're running out of time."

Chapter 4

Nathaniel walked the short distance from the office to the hotel he had checked into two days earlier. Aurora had insisted he book and check-in two full days before the first kill. She had also insisted it was expensive.

"If anything goes wrong, the authorities won't be looking for someone who booked into a top-class hotel two days earlier," she had explained. "They'll be looking for someone hurriedly checking into a cheap motel a couple of hours after the killing."

She had a point, although his bank account wasn't thanking her for the room rates, especially as he was already paying rent on his – now unoccupied – flat.

On the way from the office to the hotel, he noticed a red tinge on his hands from William's blood. He shoved his hands in his blazer pocket, which probably looked odd but he hoped people would think it was a strange affectation of a businessman rather than an attempt to conceal anything sinister. It was a short walk to the hotel, so he wouldn't have to keep his hands hidden for long. The fresh air was helping too, although images of *the body* kept flashing into his mind.

He focused his mind on the rest of his mission and also the reason for it: keeping his little girl safe.

Aurora had shown Nathaniel most of the children, but not all of them. She hadn't shown him his daughter, his little Miss Amanda. Nathaniel had told her he didn't want to see her. He believed her about the explosive devices and deliberate targeting of schools – she'd shown him the images and replayed the screams directly into his mind. She'd shown him enough to agree to the plan. He didn't need to see his little girl like that.

She had shown him the journal articles written by forensic psychologists, and various reports of the murders – the puzzling over why a group of seemingly ordinary men would inflict such horrific acts on the most innocent of society. She hadn't merely shown him crime scene photos, she'd shown him the *crime scenes*.

Those moments before the explosions were in some ways worse than the blasts. The children playing outside, oblivious to the hellfire about to be blasted upon and through them. The three men would be labelled as the worst of the worst. Named in the same breath as both the most infamous terrorists in history, and also the most despised child killers. The devastation they would leave for the families, for the few school friends who survived, for *society itself* would be felt around the world. Their names would become bywords for evil. Spoken only in hushed tones, as if the mention of their names would conjure their malevolent presence.

Arriving at the hotel, he walked straight through the lobby and took the lift to his floor. He'd been here once to check in, then once again to mess the bed up and make it look like someone was staying here. Aurora had told him it would be a good idea so he'd know the layout and look inconspicuous walking around the hotel. 'Panicked and lost' in a hotel was not a good look.

He swiped into his room with the key card and shut the door. He immediately felt a sense of relief at being safe. For now.

He went to sit on the bed.

"Wait!" Aurora blurted. "You should have a shower and change your clothes."

He nodded.

"You're right."

He waited.

"Nathaniel, you need to have a shower."

"I know, but…"

"What's wrong?"

"Can you turn around or something? It doesn't feel right you seeing me… you know."

Aurora gave a smile, and promptly disappeared.

Nathaniel undressed carefully, making sure none of his clothes touched any surface – including the floor – and threw everything straight into one of the hotel's laundry bags. Naked, he carefully sealed the laundry bag and placed it on the bed. The sheets would be changed and washed, so fibres and evidence wouldn't be a problem. At least, his limited knowledge of forensic science told him it shouldn't be.

Entering the walk-in shower, he turned the elaborate handle and allowed the warm water to cascade down from the top of his head. It felt good, although he knew that every good feeling for the rest of his life would now be experienced amidst the backdrop of an unmistakable truth. He'd crossed a line that no human ever gets to uncross. He'd killed another person.

Although could he really describe his former employee as a person, at least in the conventional sense? He was a few short months away from beginning a chain reaction of events which would lead him and his two accomplices to slaughter an untold number of children. One of which would be Nathaniel's own little Amanda. It was self-defence, a pre-emptive strike. Although the police certainly wouldn't view it that way, hence the precautions he needed to take.

He stood motionless under the shower, allowing the water to wash the dirt from his body, and hopefully anything else that a forensic scientist might be able to use.

He thought back to the first time he'd met Aurora. She'd appeared – as she so often did – out of nowhere. Nathaniel had been at his flat, having been kicked out of the family home by his wife only a short while earlier.

Sitting alone on the sofa after a full day of work, he had seen Aurora out of the corner of his eye and nearly jumped out of his skin. He'd stood up and looked around frantically as though under attack.

"Who are you?" he'd shouted at her. "How did you get in?!"

She'd looked at him with that ethereal, calming gaze and simply told him she meant him no harm. That she was a friend, that they would work together to save Amanda.

At the mention of his daughter's name he'd felt an anger rise up in him. A rage that is unique to a parent who feels their child is in danger. Nathaniel was not a violent man – not then at least – but the thought of his daughter being harmed triggered a fire deep within him.

"How do you know my daughter's name? You stay away from her!"

"Nathaniel," she had said calmly. "Please relax. Amanda is fine. She's at home with Vanessa. They're both absolutely fine. I need to talk to you about something that will happen in the future unless we take action."

"What do you mean 'we'?!" he'd shouted. "Stop saying her name!"

"Alright, Nathaniel," she'd said, again in that soothing tone. "Everything is fine. Please sit down and I will explain everything."

He'd looked at her petite frame and noticed a look in her eyes which told him she was not there to do any harm. The opposite in fact, he inexplicably felt she was there to infuse him with a sense of peace.

He'd sat back down and Aurora had explained what the future held. The men, the bombing campaign, all of it.

"But… how could you possibly know all this? *Any* of this?"

"It's not easy to explain, Nathaniel. This isn't the only place that exists."

"You mean," he asked, "you're from another universe? Like, a multiverse? That's impossible."

"Not quite, but something like that."

"That's impossible," he repeated.

"It really isn't, Nathaniel. Think about it. Is it possible I could get into this flat without opening the door or any of the windows? You know exactly which of the windows creak, as well as the exact sound they make. And we both know nobody could ever get in here without you hearing the loud click of the door lock. You made a note of it after the landlord let you in that first time, didn't you? You wondered if the loud lock would be annoying or whether it would turn out to be an effective security measure."

He stared, open-mouthed at the knowledge she had of something he had never said to another human being.

"Nathaniel, what I'm saying isn't as far-fetched as it might appear. Even Einstein had theories about different dimensions, including one where time itself was the fourth dimension. So just like you're used to moving in three dimensions – back and forward, side to side, and so on – you could move through time itself. His theory was flawed, but he was closer than anybody else has come."

"So… wait," Nathaniel said, trying to wrap his head around what he was hearing. "You're saying you're from another *dimension*? What does that even *mean*?"

"It's difficult to explain, Nathaniel. Some of the most reputable physicists believe that there are other universes with more than three dimensions. Some believe there are more than ten! They have theorised that the laws of physics are the same in each universe, but that they manifest differently to give rise to new dimensions. Do you see what I'm saying, Nathaniel? These things have been considered by scientists, philosophers and theologians for years. It's not as outlandish as it may first appear. None of it is easy to comprehend, I understand that. The important thing is that I know what will happen with these men."

"In this timeline, you mean?"

"We can call it that if you like, Nathaniel. The point is, I know what is going to happen, and I know that you are the only one who can stop it. Very few people know their purpose in life, Nathaniel. This is yours."

He stared at her, then slowly shook his head.

"This is crazy."

"I know how it seems. There are things you will need to take on faith, Nathaniel. The important thing isn't that you know everything, or what will happen next at any given time, but that you trust me."

"How am I supposed to *believe* you, let alone trust you? You're a stranger. You come into my flat – I still don't know how – and now you're telling me—"

"I'll show you."

And she did. In some middle ground between his mind's eye and the real world, he saw the news reports, the grieving families, the aftermath of the explosions.

He saw the crimes, and the perpetrators. In a few short seconds, he'd lived through, witnessed, and had horrific memories of countless atrocities.

He suddenly saw Amanda in a building and knew what was about to happen.

"Please!" he shouted. "Stop!"

In an instant the images disappeared as though they'd never existed. Although the memories remained, seared into his brain forever. He looked at Aurora.

"It's real, Nathaniel. At least, it will be. You have the chance to stop this. These men cannot be allowed to begin planning these attacks. Once they do... well, you've seen what will happen."

Standing in the shower, he thought back to all that had happened between then and now to convince him of Aurora's statements. The images she'd shown him, the sounds he'd heard, the smell of so much burning flesh... he didn't want it to be true, but she had been right about so many other things. She'd known about the dark web contact and the gun. He hadn't even known the dark web existed, let alone which software to use to access it.

She'd known about Vanessa and the arguments they'd had. Things that only they both knew. The fact Vanessa had thrown him out of the house after calling him weak. The fact she'd never thought much of him as a husband, but felt he was a good father. The fact she didn't think he was spontaneous, or dynamic, or a good protector.

Aurora had known about private conversations he'd had with Amanda. Replaying like an audio file the things he would say to her.

"Everybody loves Miss Amanda. And why does everybody love Miss Amanda? Because Miss Amanda is lovely."

Aurora knew everything that had happened, and had accurately predicted things that would happen. His raise at work, the issues that came up with suppliers that nobody could possibly have anticipated. And that was to name only two things. She'd proved herself reliable time and time again.

And the things she'd shown him… they were *real*. In some inexorable way, and somewhere in the ether, they *existed*. They weren't dreams – or nightmares — it was like a glimpse into another dimension, a different timeline. He'd had vivid dreams in his life, and he thought he had a fairly stable handle on reality. But the scenes Aurora had shown him were beyond anything he'd ever experienced. They were real events that existed somewhere. Maybe not in this universe, or dimension, or whatever other plane on which they could be described. But they were out there, and he needed to stop them. Aurora had made that clear. He was the one, the only one.

He had no choice but to believe her. How could he ignore her? His daughter's very life was at stake.

Chapter 5

Nathaniel stepped out of the shower onto the deep-pile bathroom mat, the soft material somehow managing to be cooling and warming all at the same time.

He reached over and wrapped himself in an oversized bathrobe, tying the cord around his waist and feeling cocooned. He suddenly thought of his wife, and the feel of her warm embrace. How her arms would wrap tightly around him like a protective shield against the world. Standing in the plush hotel bedroom, he longed to hold her again and smell the unique scent of her shampoo mixed with her perfume.

He checked the time, eight pm. It had been less than three hours since he had taken the life of another human being. Before his mind could register the gravity of the act, he suddenly saw an image of a burned-out school in his mind, then the roll call of pre-teen victims scrolling across the bottom of a twenty-four hour news programme.

Taken a life? Yes.

Of a human being? As before, he wasn't convinced words like 'human' or 'person' could be used with someone like that.

He walked over to the bed and lay down, mindful that he needed to keep moving to fulfil his mission, but needing a few moments of peace before starting up again. He closed his eyes and mentally ran through the plan. He would pick up the rental car – again, one he had rented and used two days ago so as to avoid detection – and would drive to the home of Ricky Gardner. Nathaniel had known Ricky for a couple of years now – he'd been on the interview panel when Ricky had got the job – so he might be briefly surprised to see Nathaniel, but would let him into the flat easily enough. Not that he was particularly concerned about that, Aurora would tell him how to get in anyway.

After Ricky, he would travel up to the conference in Birmingham and find Jonathan Owens, the final piece of this horrific jigsaw puzzle. He would then travel back down to London for his daughter's school concert, the one she had been so worried about in their earlier call.

A call which very much belonged in the 'before' section of his thoughts.

He thought of all he had to do before then, but it would be worth it. He would do anything for his Miss Amanda.

His eyes still closed, he thought of her sitting at the piano, plonking and plinking the keys with a look of determination on her face. Every so often she'd hit the right combination of notes, or press the pedal at the right time, or do something that Nathaniel wasn't really sure about, and she would look up and smile as only a child can. A grin full of pride and wonder and fun and innocence and love. *Look at me Dad! Look what I did!*

He thought back to when Amanda was a baby, and all those times when he'd come home from a long, unproductive and frustrating day at work. Feeling as though the world was a terrible place, he would walk in and see his lovely little girl and nothing else would matter for those moments. She would cry for unexplained reasons, vomit on his shoulder and face – once even up his nose – and fuss and squirm at all hours of the day and night. But even at his most exhausted and burnt-out, he knew one thing: there was nobody else he'd rather be with.

He realised very quickly what all parents find out after their first child is born but that nobody is ever told – that having children makes you both the weakest and the strongest person in the room. Strong because Nathaniel knew he would fight anyone or anything to keep her safe. He would walk into hell itself for his Miss Amanda. The consequences to him wouldn't matter. If the choice was between him being in this world, and her being in this world, he knew he would always choose her. No question.

And yet, that's what made him weak at the same time. For the rest of his life a piece of his heart walked around all by herself in this cruel, unforgiving world and no matter what he did he wouldn't be able to protect her all the time. He would always protect her when he could, of course he would, but there were times when he'd have to back off. Having children was the closest anybody got to making a voodoo doll of themselves and throwing it out into the world. No matter where you go or what you do, you can be got to. That was true for anyone a person loves of course, but the pain you feel when your child is hurt isn't a mirror like it might be for another member of the family. It's a distorted mirror in a fairground, stretching and magnifying and enlarging. You feel it somewhere else. You feel it in your soul.

Strong because of your love for your child. Weak for the very same reason.

Lying on the bed, he heard Amanda playing the piano, although wasn't sure whether it was in his mind or whether Aurora was somehow transmitting it into him. Either way, he felt an urge to move. He needed to pick up the car and be on the road in less than half an hour to stick to the plan.

He jumped off the bed and retrieved his new clothes, pausing for a second before taking off his robe to make sure Aurora wasn't in the room. She wasn't young – she was certainly older than Amanda – but it still wouldn't be appropriate for her to see him naked.

After getting dressed, he carefully took the hotel laundry bag of his old clothes and then double-bagged it with another laundry bag in case there were fibres that could be transferred to his own holdall. He hadn't known any more about forensic science than what Aurora had told him, but he was feeling paranoid. He may be fighting the good fight, but he still needed to take precautions. Nobody would understand his mission at this point, it would only be understood later on. If at all. He didn't relish what may happen, but whatever it would be was preferable to losing his little girl. He would not let that happen.

He gave a quick sweep of the room, making sure he'd got everything he needed, and made his way to check out.

***

After dropping his keys into the little box at reception, he made his way to the car park.

Stepping into the car park was a strange experience. The last time he'd been here, he had dropped off the car and gone back to his old life. There was no old life to go back to now. There was before the line was crossed, and after. That was his life now. No going back.

He opened the boot of the car and threw in the holdall, trying to be as casual as possible in case at some point in the future the CCTV was reviewed for his image. At this stage he felt fairly safe – it was likely nobody had found the body yet, so there was no need for his moves to be watched by anybody. In London everything was recorded though, and he was acutely aware that everything he did may well be played to a jury in a courtroom one day, in high definition.

His breath suddenly caught in his throat as he imagined himself in a courtroom.

"It's OK," Aurora said from behind him. "Remember why you're doing this, Nathaniel. It's more important than a courtroom. Keep going."

Her voice again had the effect of soothing him, although the knowledge of what he had done – and was about to do – still lay heavily upon him.

"I know," he whispered. "I know. For Amanda."

"For all of them, Nathaniel."

"Don't show me anything," he blurted, anticipating another round of mental images, sounds and smells, "just… just give me a moment. Please."

She placed a hand on his shoulder, and he somehow felt the warmth of her even through his clothes and jacket. Her touch had the same effect as her voice – calming.

He slowly walked around to the front of the car and got into the drivers' seat. He knew where he needed to go and had found the route earlier. He didn't want to use the satellite navigation on his phone in case he was being tracked. Again, not that he thought it was likely at this point, but why take the chance?

He had decided to avoid busy roads. It was Friday night after all, the last thing he needed was to be stuck in traffic where people could see – and possibly remember – him. He took out the printed instructions of the route and placed them on the passenger seat, for a moment wondering where Aurora would sit. It didn't matter, of course, Aurora came and went whenever she felt like it. She certainly didn't need a seat.

Taking a deep breath, he pulled out of the parking space and drove away from the hotel.

One down, he thought, two to go.

Chapter 6

Ten minutes into the drive, Nathaniel's phone rang.

He didn't want to pull over and lose momentum – or possibly be seen near his office – so he clipped on his hands-free earpiece and answered the call.

"Hello, Nathaniel Bennett."

"It's me."

The voice was too distorted to recognise as the reception was so bad.

"Sorry, who is this?"

"It's me, Nathan. Vanessa. We're married, remember?"

"Oh, sorry, Vanessa. The reception is really bad."

"Where are you?"

"I'm just driving. Why? Is everything alright?"

"I'm calling to make sure you're coming tomorrow. Amanda is telling all her friends that Mummy and Daddy are coming to the school concert, so it's really important that you come."

He bit his lip. He didn't need to be told how important it was to be there for his daughter. Of the two of them, he'd always felt like the more reliable parent.

"Of course, I'm coming," he said, managing to keep the frustration out of his voice but only just. "I told her I'd be there, so I will. I promised. It'll be fun."

She made a noise somewhere between a laugh and a grunt.

"Vanessa, I know you think I'm boring but I do like going out sometimes. And when have I ever not turned up to something Amanda is doing? You know if I say I'll be there then I will. I promised Amanda."

She didn't respond, and he took that as a small victory.

"How are things with you, Vanessa? Did they get back to you about the raise?"

"Yes, they did. I didn't get it."

"Oh. I'm sorry, Vanessa."

"It's fine," she said in a tone that told him it wasn't. "You?"

"I'm alright. I was thinking about you yesterday. Well, us. You know that place we went to by the river when we first started going out? The one with that horrible pirate-themed dinner? Well someone at work was"

"Nathan, I have to go."

"OK, sorry. Sorry, Vanessa. You go. I'll see you tomor—"

The line went dead.

He shook his head. Was that what things had come to now? Him not even being given the courtesy of being able to finish the sentence? She was trying to prove a point, of course. That she could withdraw anytime she wanted to, disappear on him without his consent. Cut him off from her, and from his daughter. The mere thought of losing Amanda caused a primal panic to surge up in him. He would do anything for her, to stay with her. It was the age-old question that fighting couples faced over and over again – can I live with this person in order to ensure I keep seeing my children? Can I put up with the barbs, the insults, the put downs, the million little chips at my own identity, if it means I get to stay with my kids?

Nathaniel knew he could. He just wasn't so sure whether Vanessa knew that she could. Not that they were in the same position. If they divorced surely Vanessa would get custody of Amanda? He didn't know much about custody battles, but from what he'd seen he was pretty sure that the Dad doesn't usually have much of a say.

He'd see Amanda every weekend maybe, or a few times through the week, maybe even every other weekend. He couldn't imagine his life in that scenario. It wouldn't be worth living. He drove a while longer, thinking about the call but trying not to, which of course meant thinking about it more than ever.

She didn't even let him finish the sentence…

A tiny little power play, a petty shot at him. Surely the separation itself was evidence that she held all the cards here?

He'd agreed to it of course, but then what choice did he have? Your wife tells you she wants a trial separation. Do you disagree so she can go ahead and file for divorce and take your little girl away from you? Or do you agree to it, and cling to the hope that in time things will go back to how they were, and you, your wife, and your little girl get to stay under the same roof? Be a family again?

Not much of a choice. Not for him anyway.

He did wonder about what Vanessa wanted from him. Maybe she wanted him to disagree, to stand up and fight. She always said he was weak, not strong or dynamic enough for her. A good father but a bad husband, she'd said, as if she were mother of the year. Not that he could fault her as a mother, or as a wife really. Which is why he'd agreed to the separation. Give her some time, show her he wasn't the weak man she thought he was, and hopefully things would go back to normal.

Although normal was the last thing Vanessa seemed to want most of the time. It was as if she was bored with the routine of life — but then who wasn't? Anybody with a mortgage, a job and a family to support have to do what they need to do to keep things going. It was never boring to Nathaniel. It was necessary and he quite liked the order of things. He liked knowing that he would finish work at a certain time and be home to see his little girl and watch television with her and Vanessa as a family. They'd eat together and talk about the day, then he'd tuck his little Amanda into bed, read her a story, and kiss her goodnight. He and Vanessa would watch television for a while, then go to sleep themselves. It was nice, comforting. What was so wrong with that?

Apparently that didn't make him spontaneous, but their teenage years were a long time ago. They were parents who lived and worked in one of the most expensive cities in the world. The mundanity and dependability of their jobs and salaries were what enabled them to live.

Thinking about his job, his mind suddenly and violently flashed back to the cupboard in his office that now housed a dead body. *The body.*

Had that been real? It didn't feel like it could've been. His memory of it felt the same as memories of films he had seen, or television shows. He wondered whether some kind of dissociation kicked in, so that reality was kept at arm's length. Not that he would mind if that was the case, he needed to use whatever resources he had to get through the rest of the mission. If he thought about it all too much he'd probably go crazy.

Driving along the dual carriageway, he wondered again how he had been able to pull the trigger. To actually do it. Three times, no less. Aurora was there, of course, and her voice always calmed him, but there was more to it than that. Maybe because he knew what was at stake? Maybe because he knew what would otherwise happen to his little Amanda?

Or maybe simply because it had all happened so quickly? There'd been so much build-up, so much planning, so much *convincing* by Aurora that this was the right thing to do, that it was possible he'd had enough time to prepare himself mentally beforehand. In fact, and this was a thought he almost didn't want to acknowledge, in some ways, it was possibly even an anti-climax. Hours and days and weeks of planning and preparing, and then it was over in a matter of seconds.

Not that it was really over, he still had two more threats to eliminate.

He liked that. Threats to eliminate. That's what they were after all, threats. Dangers that someone needed to step up and prevent. He realised that in all their conversations, Aurora had never told him why they were planning to go on and kill those children. Not that it mattered, he supposed. He was trying to stop a bombing campaign aimed at the most innocent and vulnerable in society. Would knowing why the fuses were to be lit make any difference?

He wished it could be different though. He wished he could only eliminate one threat rather than three. Aurora had been clear on that though, many times. He remembered her explaining to him late one night when his resolve wavered and he felt he must be losing his mind. Aurora was able to read him like that, knowing exactly how much information to give, and when to give it, to keep him going. Ensuring he had just what he needed, when he needed it.

"Hatred like this doesn't just switch off, Nathaniel," she had said. "If all three aren't gone then any one of them will continue. They'll find others, they'll indoctrinate them with their hatred. They'll give them enough truth to make them believe what they're saying, and then slip in lies. They'll convince others to join, and the bombings will still happen. If there was any other way then that's what we'd be doing, Nathaniel. But there isn't. As difficult as it may be to believe, this is the only way to stop this and ensure it doesn't continue through anyone else. Think of them as a three headed snake. You need to cut off all three heads or what's left will continue and grow. The only way to save those children is to get rid of all three. If you stop after one, or two, then you may as well not have started in the first place. But as soon as the bombings start, Nathaniel, you won't be able to live with yourself. Especially knowing that you could've saved Amanda."

If only Vanessa knew what he was doing. The importance of it all. And it certainly wasn't part of his daily routine, was it? He could deviate from the nine- to- five life when he needed to. When his daughter needed him to.

His phone rang again.

"Hello, Nathaniel Bennett."

"It's Vanessa."

"Oh, hello. Is everything alright?"

"Yes, it's… look, I'm sorry I had to go earlier. I'm just finding it hard to… I don't want to reminisce about things at the moment. We need space so we can decide what's best for us. We can't keep looking back to how things were. We have to… I don't know, Nathan, we have to look at how things are and try to move forward. For all our sakes."

He pulled over and switched on his hazard lights.

"I know Vanessa, I agree. I do. I want us to get back to how things were. Don't you?"

"How things were wasn't working for us, Nathan. That's what I mean, we can't just… what's the point in taking this time if nothing is going to change?"

"Just tell me what you want me to do Vanessa," he said, hearing and despising the pleading tone in his own voice. "I'll do it."

"I just need some time, Nathan," she said solemnly. "Let's just regroup and find a new way for things to be. We can't just try to get back to how things were because we'll end up here again."

"I'm sorry Vanessa, I didn't reali—"

"But there you go again, apologising. I don't need you to keep apologising."

"What *do* you need me to be?"

"Just you. Just be you. It's not about trying to be what you think I want, Nathan. I fell in love with you, Nathaniel Bennett, and I just feel like he's got lost somewhere along the way."

"I don't want to argue, Vanessa."

"I know! You never want to argue! You just want to placate me all the time and be this inoffensive, nice person to everyone."

"What's wrong with being nice?"

She sighed wearily down the phone.

"Nothing," she said sadly, "there's nothing wrong with being nice."

The silence between them yawned into a chasm, broken every so often by the occasional car racing by, which strangely seemed to exacerbate the silence. As if at the end of every sound of life they were plunged right back into death. An uncomfortable stalemate that neither of them seemed to know how to break.

"Maybe," Nathaniel finally said. "Maybe after the concert tomorrow me and you can go somewhere and talk? We can put Amanda to bed and sit in the living room."

When she spoke her voice broke.

"Nathaniel, you're not listening again. I need space. From *you*. I'm sorry, I can't... I'll see you tomorrow, Nathaniel."

"Alright, I love yo—"

The line went dead again.

He sat in the silence, allowing it to envelop him. He looked out of the window and watched life continue. Every time a car went by, he wondered about the occupants. Was it one person in there? A couple? A family? Were they happy?

That's all he wanted, his family back together again and happy.

He might not be able to do that just yet, but he knew the first step was saving Amanda. Without that, there would be no hope.

He switched off his hazard lights, flicked on the indicator, and re-joined the road. There was work to do.

Chapter 7

Ricky Gardner felt tired, but the good kind of tired.

Not stressed-out-tired, or haven't-slept-because-the-mattress-is-lumpy-tired, but been-to-the-gym-and-had-a-good-workout-tired.

He'd managed a new personal best on the treadmill, spent enough time on the rowing machine to get from here to Spain, and then topped it all off with a full kettlebell class. His arms and legs felt like jelly – and it pretty much hurt to breathe at this point – but he felt satisfied.

He wasn't bulky – a previous girlfriend had described him as wiry – but he was strong, had stamina, and – most importantly – could show off his abdominal muscles on holiday. Not that he'd had one of those recently.

He lay back on his sofa, groaning as his tired body – *good* tired – resisted the movement. He reached over to the oversized plastic beaker on the armrest, and sipped his protein shake, trying to fool himself that it didn't taste like burnt cocoa. He'd bought two kilos of it – pretending it tasted OK was the preferable option to throwing it all out.

The television was on but he wasn't really watching it. Occasionally he'd binge-watch a television show recommended to him, but in the main it was on so the flat didn't feel so empty. He was between flatmates – and between girlfriends if we're having that conversation – so more often than not, the only other voices in the flat belonged to fictional characters on television shows. That or the obligatory conference calls he had with work colleagues when he worked from home. Speaking of which, he needed to call William. Not tonight, obviously, it was Friday so he was probably out somewhere or having a night in with his girlfriend or something. He'd call him tomorrow.

He sipped some more of his protein drink and glanced at the TV. Some news report had come on about yet more budget cuts. When would people learn? There were too many people in this country, of course there had to be budget cuts! Get rid of some of the people and the problem is solved. It wasn't rocket science, it was basic mathematics. If there is x amount of money and 100 times x amount of people, then something has to give. Less people means more resources. Hospitals wouldn't be overstretched, paramedics would be able to get to the people that actually needed help so they wouldn't die on the floor of their own home after waiting two hours for help that was never going to come in the first place…

He looked up at the photo on the wall. His dad smiled back at him, blissfully unaware that a few months later he'd be living and dying in a domestic nightmare. Three years had passed now, but Ricky was still as raw as he'd been when he'd first heard the news.

"Love you, Dad," he said to the photo, before lifting his protein shake as if expecting his father to clink glasses with him.

His focus was broken by the sound of a herd of feet running past his front door, accompanied by squeals and giggling. He shook his head. Why couldn't people control their fucking kids? It was nearly ten o'clock at night, why were they even *awake* let alone running up and down the corridors in the apartment block?

He angrily reached for the remote control and winced as the movement sent a jolt through his arm. He pushed the Volume Up button so hard he heard the remote crack slightly, then switched to a music channel. He chose jazz, which was loud enough to drown out the annoying kids, but calm enough to help him rest. Little shits. Why don't they go play on a busy road instead?

He rolled his shoulder around to try to relive the pain in his arm.

He closed his eyes and sipped his shake. Sometimes he gulped it all down in only a few seconds, like a college student at a frat party. He honestly thought he'd start gagging if he did that tonight. Some days the protein shake tasted worse than others, and today was one of those days unfortunately. Still, it could've been worse, he'd tried downing raw egg yolks at one stage but couldn't stomach more than two. And even then he threw them back up shortly afterwards.

Still with his eyes closed, he put down the shake and lay back onto the sofa, allowing it to take his weight so his aching body wouldn't have to. The music was helping, but he could still hear the kids in the corridor. Little shits. Fuck them and their useless parents.

Chapter 8

Nathaniel drove down Ricky's street and slowed the car to a crawl as he looked for the right apartment block. There were four which had all been made by the same developer so all looked exactly the same, so the only way to differentiate was to slow right down and squint, which didn't feel like the smartest thing to do for obvious reasons. Aurora wasn't with him so he couldn't rely on her telling him.

He identified what looked like the right building and indicated to turn into one of the free spaces at the front.

"No," Aurora said, suddenly appearing in the passenger seat and causing him to jump almost out of the roof of the car.

"Don't *do* that," he blurted. "I'm on edge already here."

"Sorry," she said quietly. "But don't park in front of the building. Keep going and turn right into the second side street. There's a space behind a parked lorry which you should park behind."

"OK," he said, not knowing if he felt calmer because of Aurora's voice or because he'd recovered from being scared shitless.

He followed her instructions and, sure enough, there was a space just big enough for his car behind a huge lorry. From the top of the street he couldn't even see the lorry, let alone the space behind it. He'd just trusted Aurora, which had once again paid off.

After parking the car, he went to open the door.

"Wait," Aurora said, "before you get out, Nathaniel, there are a few things I need to tell you. Firstly, try not to touch anything any more than you have to. When you need to touch a handle try and use your sleeve instead of your hand, or one of the tissues in the glove compartment. This isn't like your office where your fingerprints can be easily explained. There is no reason for you to be here, or to ever have visited realistically, so we need to be careful. Once you get in, there'll be a lift that'll take you to the third floor where Ricky lives. When you press the buttons, even then use a tissue or your sleeve. You could even use your knuckle, although that's not ideal. Where is the gun?"

"In my jacket," Nathaniel said solemnly, suddenly feeling a surge of adrenalin.

"It's OK, Nathaniel," Aurora said, as if sensing his rising panic. "Remember that you're saving lives. You're on the right side of this war, Nathaniel."

It doesn't feel like it, he thought.

"I know it doesn't," Aurora said gently. "But this *is* a war, Nathaniel. Soldiers don't choose what orders they are given, but they do what they need to. What they know is right. You know the stakes, Nathaniel. You can do this. Look how far you've already come."

For once, her voice wasn't having the calming effect that it usually did. It was all very well telling him he was on the right side, but he was the one risking jail or worse. He was the one going out and killing people. He was the one pulling the trig—

All at once he was transported to the aftermath of one of the bombings. He knew his body was still in the car, but it was as immersive an experience as it could've been given that he knew he was physically somewhere else.

He stood in the silence. People always talk about the calm before the storm, but nobody ever mentions the calm after it. Those moments after evil has visited, sending shock waves through the ground and scorching the sky. Those moments where the very earth is collecting itself and trying to understand the violations that have been wrought upon it.

He looked around in horror, taking in the horrific sight of small bodies strewn around the remains of what must have been a school. In an instant the world erupted into sound again, as the firefighters and police arrived and witnessed the carnage of the scene – smouldering rubble and little bodies.

Then Nathaniel was launched forward through time. He saw huddled couples staring into the ruins of the school, as if it would somehow either confirm or deny their worst fears about their children. The pain and fear on their faces was tangible, the tears streaming from their bloodshot eyes and falling relentlessly to the ash-covered ground. They held each other, as if anchoring themselves in this, the most horrific of stormy seas. A situation forcing them to question how something like this could happen, why it would happen, and why their poor, innocent child should be the recipient of such random, merciless evil. Nathaniel could see the fundamental question asked and answered on their faces.

Was this real?

Yes, it was.

More real than their minds could process.

He could see them trying to comprehend, asking themselves questions which they weren't able to answer. What did this mean for them and the tiny bed, the colourful duvet cover, the favourite soft toys sitting in their child's bedroom at home?

In an instant, Nathaniel was back in the car.

He felt Aurora's hand on his own.

"I know it's you who is risking everything, Nathaniel," she said kindly. "You just have to stay focused on *why* you're doing it at all. You can stop these horrors from becoming reality, Nathaniel. Only you. You are the only solider on this battlefield who can end the war."

"But, why?" he asked. "How can I possibly be the only one? The only person in the world who can stop that?"

"You have to trust me, Nathaniel. You are the only one. Without you, those children have no hope."

"But, I know you said that they'd still go ahead if there were only two of them, or even just one left. But... how can that be true?"

"Nathaniel, I know how you feel but please remember what I told you when we first met. If there was any other way that we could stop this, then that's what we would do. It has to be all three of them. It has to be soon. And," she squeezed his hand, "it has to be you."

The images and sounds were still with him. In some terrible future that, apparently, he was the only one who could stop. He saw the parents, holding onto each other for dear life. Pleading with who or whatever they believed in that it wouldn't be true, that their child would be the one to be miraculously spared.

"The first one was the hardest and you did it, Nathaniel. *You did it*," Aurora continued. "You only have to do this two more times and countless lives will be saved."

He looked into her face, there was nothing but kindness in it.

"Amanda will be saved," she said softly.

He felt something galvanise in his soul, as a clarity cut through the noise in his mind. His mission was clear, he'd known it from the start. He just needed reminding. It wouldn't make the act any easier, but it would mean he'd follow it through, no matter what.

Inexplicably his mind flashed back to the conversation with Vanessa, but he pushed it out of his mind. It served no purpose now, he had to focus on what he had to do. Dwelling on the problems he and Vanessa were having was simply a distraction.

He picked up his jacket and got out of the car.

Standing behind the lorry and feeling shielded from any prying eyes, he carefully put on his jacket and patted the pocket containing the gun. It was solid, reassuring. He knew Ricky kept himself in shape, he just hoped he'd get the chance to use the gun before Ricky was able to stop him.

Chapter 9

Nathaniel took a deep breath and walked towards the front door of the building. Looking in, he'd expected to see a front desk and a receptionist, but there was nobody. There wasn't even an intercom system, so Nathaniel stepped in purposefully and headed straight for the lift.

As Aurora had instructed, he used his sleeve to press the lift call button, wondering how that would look if the CCTV was ever checked. Would he look like an eccentric resident? A visitor with a fear of germs? Maybe. He just hoped none of the cameras were monitored in real-time, and that anything that was recorded would be deleted by the time anyone had discovered anything. He knew a lot of places looped their security footage so it was only kept for twenty-four hours or so.

The lift arrived and he stepped into the metal box, suddenly realising for the first time in his life how claustrophobic and restrictive they could be. A reinforced metal structure smaller than a prison cell. At least prison cells had windows... Lift doors close securely and once they start moving nobody can get in – or out – no matter how hard they try.

He hurriedly pressed the floor button – again with his sleeve.

The doors began to creep together slowly, then suddenly clanged shut, as though they had been offering him a chance of escape but then had changed their mind and decided to lock him in.

A wave of claustrophobia playfully swept over him, although it seemed to leave as quickly as it had come. It was a fleeting panic which caused a momentary feeling of breathlessness, but it then dissipated harmlessly into the air. Like a predator scared off by an even bigger one.

He looked behind him. Aurora had her hand on his shoulder.

She didn't speak, but held his gaze as the lift travelled up towards Ricky Gardner's doom. He looked into those eyes, so deep and mysterious, and yet somehow so familiar and comforting. Like walking into an alien land yet inexplicably feeling right at home. It reminding him of holding his newborn child – unfathomable and confusing, yet so much a part of himself it couldn't help but feel familiar.

He thought of his Amanda, and once again felt his determination harden. He broke eye contact with Aurora, and took another look at the metal walls around him. His viewpoint had changed now. He had steel running through his veins – these walls couldn't hold him even if they'd wanted to.

The lift gave a small beep as it stopped at the floor, and the doors opened as slowly as they had done before. Not teasing this time though. Timid. As though they knew the frame of mind of the occupant and wanted him to leave without incident.

Walking out of the lift, he realised that he didn't feel worried anymore, although at the same time he wasn't filled with overconfidence either. He recognised the feeling as how he usually felt before business meetings – prepared, and with a job to do. He absent mindedly patted the gun, and walked over to Ricky's flat.

He knocked on the door and as he waited he heard the faint sounds of a trumpet being played. He hadn't pegged Ricky as a jazz fan, but then he didn't know him that much at all. He only really knew what Aurora had shown him, the rest had been short meetings here and there, and virtual meetings online.

He heard the floorboards creak as – he assumed – Ricky walked over to the door. He heard the clang of a deadbolt being unlocked, then the jingle of keys before the unmistakable click of the door being unlocked.

Ricky yanked opened the door and for a brief moment Nathaniel saw something unexpected in his face. Anger.

"Oh," he said. "Nathaniel? I mean, Mr Bennett."

He leaned out of the door and looked down the hall as though expecting someone else.

"What, um, are you doing here?"

"Sorry to disturb you at home, Ricky. Have you got a second? It won't take long, I promise."

"Um," Ricky glanced again down the corridor. "Yeah, of course. Come in."

Nathaniel stepped into the flat.

"Sorry," Ricky said, "I thought you were… kids are always running up and down the corridor so I thought maybe it was them knocking on the door."

Kids, Nathaniel thought, and the images Aurora had shown him flashed into his mind. He knew it wasn't Aurora putting them there this time, it was his own mind remembering what she'd shown him.

"You don't like children?" Nathaniel asked, trying to be casual but hoping that Ricky would give something away, or make an inappropriate comment, something that would show his true colours to him. As prepared as he felt, things would be easier if he could connect the Ricky that Aurora had shown him with the one standing in front of him.

"No, it's… you know how it is. Sometimes you just want some quiet, yeah? Would you like a drink Mr Bennett?"

"Oh no, I won't stay long. Thanks Ricky. Actually, would you mind if I used your bathroom? Sorry, I've been in the car for a while."

"Yes, no problem. Let me show you."

Ricky took Nathaniel to what was possibly the dingiest bathroom he had ever seen. It was obvious Ricky lived alone, the top of the sink looked like a science experiment to investigate mould growth on old splashes of toothpaste. The bath wasn't much of an improvement, and the less said about the toilet bowl the better.

Nathaniel locked the door and sat on the side of the bath. He was still wearing his coat, which enabled him to slip his hand into the inside pocket and retrieve the gun. He checked it was loaded, although knew there was no possibility that he would've forgotten to do so. The suppressor was still fitted, and it was quiet enough for him to use in a block of flats. At least, he hoped it was.

Maybe he could ask Ricky to turn the music up?

The real issue was how to do it. Nathaniel knew that Ricky was in good shape, so it was unlikely he'd get the chance to overpower him. He needed to take him by surprise somehow. He certainly couldn't risk a stand-off as

Ricky would likely get to him first, or – possibly even more dangerously – would start making noise and alert other people.

Something else niggled at him too.

The flat was just that, a flat. There was no indication of anything to do with bombs or terrorism. Yes, he'd mentioned children, but that was hardly concrete proof. He trusted Aurora – more than he trusted himself a lot of the time – but if he could just *see* something, some little indication that Ricky would truly go on to do what Aurora said he would, then he'd feel more justified.

He wondered why he hadn't felt that way earlier. Although Nathaniel had never seen the home of his first 'threat', so was free to imagine it as a dark, dingy place full to the rafters with chemicals, detonators and blocks of explosive. From what he had briefly seen of Ricky's flat, this was no evil genius' lair. It was more bachelor pad than anything. The type of place Nathaniel had seen before, had *inhabited* before. Without the mess, obviously.

There was a soft knock on the door.

"Nath— um, Mr Bennett. Are you OK?"

"I'm fine, Ricky," Nathaniel said, hastily putting the gun back in his coat pocket. He flushed the toilet and walked over to the sink, grimacing as his fingers slipped on something greasy on the tap. He washed his hands.

Thoroughly. The towel was damp and discoloured, so he wiped his hands on his clothes instead.

He unlocked the door and stepped out.

"Sorry, Ricky," he said calmly.

"That's alright. Do you want to sit down?"

"Yes, thanks."

They walked into the living area and Nathaniel took in the view. It was tidier than he had expected, and smelled surprisingly like sweet vanilla. There was a huge leather sofa against one wall, and on the opposite was a gargantuan television, which Nathaniel saw was the a source of the music. The television actually covered a good third of the window.

In-between the two was a rectangular coffee table. Again, Nathaniel was surprised at how clean it all looked. On a glass coaster sat a large plastic beaker half- full of what looked like milkshake, and a remote control next to it, but other than that, the table was empty, and spotless.

He wondered what the best next move would be. Should he actually sit down? He would need to at some point, otherwise he'd look suspicious just standing in the middle of the room. But then what? He sits down, and *then what?* He was used to plans and strategies, not improvising.

"Take a seat, Mr Bennett."

Too late. He didn't have a choice now.

Unless…

He casually walked over to the window and pulled back a curtain. He could buy some time like this.

"What kind of view do you have from up here?" he asked, trying to keep his voice casual. He looked out.

"Wow," he continued. It's really nice."

"Nathaniel."

"Yes," he said, turning round.

Ricky looked at him blankly.

"What's that?" Ricky asked.

"Did you… Didn't you just say my name?"

"Your name? No, I… Wait, did you say, yes?"

"I thought you…" Ricky started, before realising it wasn't Ricky's voice he'd heard. It was Aurora's.

"Never mind," he said quietly, and turned back to the window. He suddenly felt the need to pat the gun again, but thought better of it.

Aurora's voice returned, louder and stronger this time.

"Knock over the beaker."

He frowned. A question ricocheted around his mind. Do *what?*

"Knock over the beaker, then he'll bend down to pick it up. Then you've got your chance."

"Mr Bennett," Ricky said, "would you mind letting me know what this is about please? I am quite tired and it's, well, it's Friday night."

"Of course, Ricky," Nathaniel said, turning round and smiling. "Maybe we *should* sit down."

"Please do," Ricky said, and gestured to the sofa.

Time slowed to a crawl for the next couple of seconds, as Nathaniel walked towards the sofa and aimed himself at the corner where the beaker sat. As he walked he realised he was nowhere near it, and would have to leap to the right if he had any chance of knocking it over. He veered over but it was no good, he wouldn't make it. Not without looking obvious.

He reached the sofa and sat down, moving himself along so that his body was closer to the corner of the table. If he could just knock it somehow... Maybe with his foot? Or his knee? He just needed to reach it and give a little push so it'd fall onto the floor and Ricky would have to clean it.

"So, Ricky," he said, trying to give his voice an authoritative edge. "I want to thank you for letting me in. As you said, it's Friday evening and I'm sure we'd both rather not talk about work."

Ricky smiled politely, but Nathaniel could see the strain in it. Yes, he'd been one of the interview panel who had hired Ricky, but he got the feeling Ricky wouldn't be polite much longer. And from what Aurora had said about him, Nathaniel didn't want to be there to see him turn angry.

Chapter 10

Nathaniel had to think of something, and fast. This was taking too long and it was showing on the face of his host.

"So, Ricky," he said as good-naturedly as he could muster, "as you know we're looking to expand where we can. We've had a good quarter, in fact, we've had a few good years. Consecutively, too. So that means expansion and opportunities. In short, it means a lot of people will be moving up."

He inched his body closer to the table. If he stretched underneath he might *just* be able to kick one of the legs and send the beaker over.

"And I'm sure that you know we often look for people to promote at times like this. People who we've seen have got real potential."

He simultaneously shuffled on the seat as though getting comfortable and shot his foot out at the table leg.

It didn't budge.

"Oops, sorry," he said, feeling both deflated and panicked in equal measure.

"It's OK," Ricky said. "You were saying something about promotions?"

"Yes, er... where was I? I'd forget my head if it wasn't screwed on. That's an odd expression isn't it? Who has a head that screws on? I don't, and I don't know anybody else that does either. Ha!"

Ricky rubbed his forehead. Nathaniel could see he was getting agitated now, and finding it harder to hide. Or less necessary.

"Who is getting promoted, Mr Bennett?"

"Well, nothing has been decided yet, but I was wondering if you would be interest—"

He shuffled again and gave the table a harder kick, knocking the beaker slightly but not hard enough to come off the table.

"Sorry," he said again, "I'm not sure what's wrong with me today."

"It's fine," Ricky said, reaching over and moving the beaker onto the floor next to his foot. Nathaniel almost groaned. What was he supposed to do now?

And where was Aurora?

"Don't worry, Mr Bennett. You were wondering if I'd be interested in...?"

"If you'd be interested, yes. In a promotion."

"Well, yes, of course. Definitely. I mean, what would be the actual job title?"

Nathaniel suddenly realised he didn't even know Ricky's current job title. He couldn't say something lower or on the same level, obviously, but he also couldn't go too high or it'd be obvious he was lying. If Ricky was a sales executive, he wouldn't be offered a director of marketing job, would he?

"Sorry, Ricky, would you mind if I did have a drink please? Just water would be fine if that's OK. Then we can finish talking. I've got a bit of a frog in my throat. That's another funny expression isn't it? A frog in your throat!"

Ricky stared at Nathaniel for a second – a second too long Nathaniel felt – and nodded.

"No problem," he said, getting up and immediately knocking the beaker onto the floor. It didn't so much spill as erupt.

"Shit!" Ricky said, before rushing out of the room and saying something about a towel.

"Now is your chance, Nathaniel," Aurora said. "He's going to come back with tissues and try to clean the floor. When he does, you have your chance. But you'll have three or four seconds at most. Don't miss the chance."

The adrenalin flooded Nathaniel and he stood up quickly, ready to retrieve the gun. He was going to do it. He was actually going to pull the trigger on a second person.

"Not person," Aurora said, interrupting his thoughts. "Remember? Remember what they are going to do. How many lives they are going to destroy."

Nathaniel hesitated. He wished he didn't have to keep being reminded over and over in order to do the things he needed to do. It would be so much simpler if Aurora convinced him the first time, and that was it. If he only needed to be persuaded once and that trust, that faith in the fact he was doing the right thing would carry him through the rest of this mission. He felt like he needed constant reminding.

He looked at Aurora.

"Show me something," he whispered. "I won't be able to do it otherwi—"

Immediately, Aurora projected the image of a man in a grey suit into his mind. He sat in a plush office and looked to Nathaniel like either a lawyer or stockbroker. He was sitting behind a desk and holding a phone to his ear. Nathaniel heard the unmistakable words coming from the handset, "I'm so sorry, but Jade was one of the victims." The man's face changed from a concerned parent maintaining professionalism in the face of a stressful situation into a rictus of raw, primal agony. Tears streamed down his face and he grabbed at the photo on his desk. A young girl – Amanda's age – smiled back at him. He howled as he brought the picture to his chest, all composure gone. Nathaniel suddenly felt his pain as if it were his own. He felt tears prick his own eyes suddenly, as he saw the memories of this man's daughter flash through his mind. Her first steps, her first words, her first day at nursery, the food she loved – and hated – the television adverts she laughed at even though she wasn't possibly old enough to understand the jokes, the cuddles she wanted when she was ill, when she wasn't. The promise of all that she could and would become. All of it, gone. Ripped away in the flash and searing heat of an explosion.

An explosion caused by the man who now rushed into the living room with a handful of wadded tissues in one hand, and a bath towel in the other.

He crouched down and began mushing the tissues into the mess. The thin paper stuck to the viscous liquid, quickly dissolving into it and creating a thick paste. Ricky continued mashing at it, assumedly in the hope that it would suddenly start cleaning the mess.

"Fucking thing," he said angrily. "Piece of fucking shit. Fucking protein tastes like shit too."

Nathaniel whipped the gun out from his coat pocket.

"Three seconds," Aurora said.

He aimed the weapon at the back of Ricky's head, swallowing hard and steeling himself for the shot.

"Two seconds, Nathaniel."

The gun was primed, loaded. Ready.

Nathaniel wasn't sure if he was.

"Do it, Nathaniel! One second."

Nathaniel felt tears in his eyes and blinked them away. He scrunched up his eyes and shook his head slightly in an attempt to clear his now-blurred vision.

Ricky turned his head and looked up, an expression of shock and raw horror on his face.

"What the—"

Panicking, Nathaniel fired. As with the first target, the noise was minimal but the impact huge. The bullet entered Ricky's temple, jerking his head awkwardly and causing a sick, red explosion from the other side of his face. Ricky dropped to the floor at the exact moment Nathaniel stepped back and somehow fell backwards onto the sofa.

He kept the gun trained on Ricky, who lay motionless.

Ricky's gaze was fixed on Nathaniel. The light behind the eyes was rapidly diminishing, but the eyes themselves stared at Nathaniel, boring holes into his skull as totally as the bullet had bored a hole into his own.

Nathaniel knew that no matter what, this moment would stay burned into his brain forever.

Blood seeped from Ricky's head and pooled onto the floor, creeping towards the mixture of wet tissue and milkshake, before slowly infusing into it. Like two bodies of water – one crimson, one white – suddenly meeting and creating a sickly pink mess.

"Leave, Nathaniel," Aurora said quietly but urgently.

He looked from Ricky – who was surely dead now, there was nothing behind the eyes – and towards Aurora.

"There is no time," she continued with an authority he hadn't remembered hearing before. "Nobody has seen you so far. But you have to leave now."

He turned back to Ricky and stared, unblinking.

In an instant Nathaniel felt Aurora pushing more thoughts into his head. More images, more horrors.

"No!" he said, awakening from his trance. "Please. No more death. Not now... please."

He felt her hand on his forehead. It was a soothing sensation, reminding him of his mother checking his temperature when he was a small boy.

"I know what this feels like, Nathaniel. But you have to get out of here now. Nobody has seen you. There is nothing to tie you to this property. The company who monitor the security cameras are experiencing problems in their workforce, and so this footage will not be reviewed until after it is wiped over again. You have to leave *right now*. You cannot give them a reason to review the footage any earlier than they should."

Nathaniel looked at the gun still in his hand.

"Nathaniel!" Aurora screamed into his mind, somehow louder than any audible noise in the real world. He winced as though an electric shock had been shot into him.

Nathaniel snapped out of his fugue state, and looked around as if seeing the room for the first time. He shuffled off the sofa, being careful to avoid stepping near the body. Or what was left of it.

As he pushed down on the sofa to get to a standing position, he felt a dull pain in his wrist as though he'd put too much weight on it. Aurora had told him a lot of things, but she'd apparently neglected to tell him about the gun's recoil.

He put the gun away, stepped over to the front door and carefully unlocked it with his sleeve. Already feeling relived he would no longer have to look at the mess he'd made, he began to pull the door open.

"Wait!" Aurora said. "Stop!"

He heard footsteps running along the corridor, then the unmistakable sound of giggling children. He slowly pushed the door closed, stifling a wince as the pain in his wrist shot through him, and waited.

He didn't dare breathe.

An eternity later another door on the same floor opened and closed, and the sounds in the corridor stopped.

He looked over at Aurora. She nodded.

"Quickly," she added.

He yanked open the door, stepped through and closed it silently. He made his way back to the lift. Not running, but not exactly strolling either.

He pushed the button with his sleeve, making a mental note to buy some gloves for next time, and waited. His heart beat a tattoo in his chest, and his clothes felt too tight around his neck and his stomach. The lift finally arrived, and he stepped in quickly, pushing the green 'G' with his elbow and trying not to tremble.

The doors closed with their now-customary rhythm – slowly creeping towards each other before a final, rapid clang – and he stood in the centre of the lift with his hands in his pockets and his head down.

The rumble and vibration of the lift mirrored his own trembling body.

"Nearly there, Nathaniel," Aurora said. "You're doing well."

The lift pinged as it reached the ground floor, and Nathaniel braced himself as the doors opened. Surely there'd be someone there now? Maybe they'd gone for their break earlier, or maybe they'd helped one of the residents for a few minutes. Either way, they could be back by now. All it would take is one person to see him…

The doors opened.

Nobody there.

There was no time to be relieved – it was still possible a person would arrive at any moment. He rushed across the floor, keeping his head down through sheer paranoia, and pushed open the front door with his shoulder.

He didn't look around as he stepped out of the building. He locked his attention onto the side street where he'd parked and marched towards it.

Arriving at the car, he opened the door and got into the driver's seat. He locked the doors and allowed the silence and the darkness to envelop him. If the lift was a prison cell, this metal box was an escape pod.

For what felt like the first time since pulling the trigger, he allowed himself to breathe.

Chapter 11

Vanessa poured more wine into her glass. Unsteadily.

"Woah, Ness!" her friend, Shaye exclaimed. "What's the rush?"

"No rush. I'm celebrating," she said, passing the full glass of wine to Shaye.

"And what, pray tell, are we celebrating?"

Vanessa shrugged.

"It's Friday. And work is over for another week. And I've got my very good friend in my living room and we're watching a terrible film and drinking hopefully not terrible wine. My beautiful daughter who hates going to bed is finally fast asleep upstairs. What's not to celebrate?"

Shaye smiled and gave her friend a sad look.

"You really should say something to them, you know."

"I know," Vanessa said, pouring wine into her own glass. "But what exactly can I say? I asked them for a raise, I didn't get it. Begging isn't going to help. C'est la vie."

"But you do so much, Ness. You deserve more."

"Oh, I deserve more in a lot of areas! Seriously though, what can you do? I feel lucky I've even got a job at this point, look at Yvonne. Three kids, and they have to get by on only her husband's salary now. They've just bought a new house too."

"I know, Ness. I'm just saying. You're worth more."

"I'm not going to disagree, but enough talk, let's drink!"

They clinked glasses and had some wine. Shaye sipped, Vanessa gulped.

"Speaking of which," Shaye said in a tone somewhere between *concerned* and *nosy*. "How's everything with the separation? Have you heard from Nathan?"

"He called earlier. I think I was a bit rude but I wasn't in the mood for walks down memory lane. I need space. And that's not particularly easy with Amanda. He wants to be involved with her."

"But that's a good thing."

"Oh, I know. It's better than him not caring. It just means I can't have a proper break. It'd probably be good for both of us. We've got the concert tomorrow so I'll see him then."

Vanessa looked at the television and tuned in to the film they'd put on. She hadn't really been watching so wasn't sure what was going on. It looked like some kind of love triangle was going on, and the main character kept switching from a New York City accent to a bad English one. At one point she was dressed as a maid, it all looked pretty wacky and not very funny. She hadn't been following, but it didn't matter. The main thing she needed tonight was a friend, not a storyline that she could follow.

She turned to Shaye and caught her friend staring at her.

"What?" she said, gently touching her lips. "Have I got wine on my face or something?"

"No, you haven't. I'm just… Are you doing OK, Vanessa? Be honest with me."

Vanessa nodded. Even to her it felt unconvincing.

"I mean, I miss Nathan. And Amanda needs him. I just don't miss the type of person I become around him. Do you know what I mean? He needs me to constantly tell him what to do and it's just exhausting, Shaye. He's so good with Amanda, but with me he's…"

She paused, and took another gulp of wine.

"I suppose it's like he's a great father to our daughter, but then he needs me to be his mother. Does that make sense?"

Shaye nodded.

"He's… I love him but it's like I have to become this 'parent' around him all the time. And I know that I am a parent, obviously, but I'm Amanda's parent, not Nathan's. I just wish he'd take charge and be more, I don't know…"

"Dynamic?"

"Yes, dynamic. Or, oh I don't know, a bit more spontaneous. He's never booked a surprise weekend away for us – before Amanda was born I mean, I wouldn't expect him to do it now. But with him everything's always so planned and ordered. I get bored with the routine of home, work, home, work, et cetera. But it's like that's what he lives for. I suppose…"

She took a sip of wine, but didn't continue talking this time. She looked again at the television, two totally unfamiliar characters were limbo dancing at a beach party.

"What?" Shaye finally asked.

"I suppose I just feel like I need more than that. More than him. Oh, I don't know. Is that really what I want? I don't know, Shaye, I really don't. I want *something*, and I don't feel like it's this. I remember when we met each other. We were in a bar and he was the only person there wearing a tie. Everyone else was casual, or at least not as formal, but he just stood there wearing his smart tie and touching it every so often to make sure it hadn't moved. I thought it was sweet then, that little check every so often, but maybe it was just his nerves at being out of the house, or weakness or something. Not that he isn't sweet, he is, but it's like he needs a kick up the arse sometimes to get him moving. If I hadn't got pregnant with Amanda two minutes after the wedding I wonder how long it would've taken us to decide to have kids. Do you know what I mean? That's why I asked him to move out for a while. I need to decide, one way or another."

"What if you decide it's better with him living somewhere else?"

Vanessa sighed.

"Then," she said, raising her glass. "I really will need to drink."

"Seriously, Ness."

"I don't know, Shaye. I'm just not sure I want to be married to a great dad and a mediocre husband."

The words hung in the air between them. They sipped more wine and watched the TV in silence for a while.

"Do you regret marrying him?" Shaye asked hesitantly.

"I don't regret it, Shaye. If I wasn't with him we wouldn't have Amanda. Although…"

She lowered her voice.

"Sometimes," she continued, "I do feel trapped. If it was just me and Nathan, it'd be easier if we ever… If things didn't work. But with Amanda… I don't want her growing up thinking her parents hate each other."

"The thing is, Ness, if you're in the same house and fighting all the time, that's exactly what she will think."

"But I *don't* hate him. I don't. I just feel as though… Do you ever step outside your life and watch it slipping right by you? I love Amanda, and I think I still love Nathan. But they're both keeping me here in this life, does that make sense?"

The look on Shaye's face told Vanessa that it probably didn't.

"I just mean," she continued, "that sometimes I look at other people – single people, without kids – and think about what else I could be doing. Does that make me a bad mum?"

"No, Ness, it makes you human. Everybody looks around and wonders what else could be. It's normal. It's obvious how much you love Amanda, and don't you dare wonder if you're a good mum. You're the best. But you're human, Ness, and you're responsible for the well-being of another human. Of course, it's going to feel too hard sometimes! If I had the emotional, psychological and physical welfare and development of another person to deal with I'd probably go mad."

"Thanks, Shaye. It's just so hard going through this with Nathan and having to be strong for Amanda at the same time. She needs her daddy. Unfortunately, I'm just not sure I do."

She gulped another mouthful of wine and turned back to the television. A new character had arrived now, carrying what looked like a bunch of plastic flowers in one hand and a miniature podium in the other.

"Are you following this film?" Shaye asked, laughing too hard and sounding to Vanessa like someone trying to be 'normal'. "I literally have no idea what's going on."

"Me neither, Shaye. Me neither."

Chapter 12

Nathaniel clenched his fist a few times and shook his hand, trying to assuage the pain in his wrist.

It had been a full hour – and almost fifty miles – since he had left the flat. And *the body*. As he entered the motorway service station he wondered how long he'd have to drive after all this was over to get away from it once and for all. A lot further than Birmingham, he imagined.

Aurora had convinced him that he needed to eat something, in spite of the ever-growing knotted rope that seemed to have replaced his stomach. Not wanting to argue, and knowing that she was right and that he did need to keep his strength up, he'd pulled up at the motorway services. It wasn't one of the nicer places – there were no recognisable food logos or smiling mascots staring at him – but that was fine for him. He wanted somewhere dingy, somewhere quick, and most of all somewhere anonymous. Families and anyone who had time to spare would go to the nicer motorway services, although in Nathaniel's experience nice motorway services were pretty oxymoronic.

He walked over to the counter and ordered a vague approximation of fish pie. Every time he looked at the food behind the plexiglass on the counter, he'd had to physically stop himself from retching. There was some kind of chicken curry and burnt coasters which were supposed to be hamburgers, but he'd passed on both. Meat was not something he had any desire to eat. Possibly ever again.

As he wasn't hungry, it really didn't matter what he ordered. As he lifted the tray of food, a sharp pain shot through his wrist, causing his flat cola to nearly spill out of the flimsy paper cup. They'd run out of lids, of course.

He walked slowly to a plastic table in the corner of the empty food court, propping up one side of the tray with his elbow rather than his hand so as to stop the pain from kicking in again. He sat down and began taking small mouthfuls of food at a time, so as not to gag. It didn't taste bad to be fair, but his whole body felt tight and clenched.

He might be doing the right thing, but it certainly didn't feel very good right now. He had faith in Aurora, and knew as far as he could that he was on the right side. That was the thing about faith though – it sometimes meant continuing on in spite of yourself.

He sipped some of his flat cola, picking up the cup with his good hand, and watched a cleaner at the other end of the food court mopping up the detritus from the previous hundred customers. The cleaner methodically sprayed what must have been detergent on the floor, left it for around 30 seconds, then squeezed out the excess water from the mop before swishing it expertly across the floor. Then he repeated the exact same process, over and over again. It was hypnotic. The same amount of detergent, the same length of time, the same amount of water, the same smooth figure-of-eight swishes. Then, a sparkling piece of flooring, and a quick move to the next section.

He thought back to the mess around *the body* at the flat, then the blood pulsing out of *the body* back in his office. He wished every mess could be mopped up as easily.

The last time he sat eating by himself on a plastic chair at a plastic table was when Vanessa was in labour. They'd told him he had a short window before anything might potentially happen, so he should take the opportunity to go and get some food. Those were some of the last few hours of his life before his daughter was born. It was strange thinking back to that time. He had been alive a full twenty-eight years before Amanda was born, and yet whenever he thought back to times in his adult life it was as if she'd always been there. At one point he'd spent a full five minutes trying to work out who had been babysitting Amanda at his twenty-fifth birthday party.

The time before his daughter was born felt strange just seconds after she had arrived into the world. Everything was the same, of course, yet everything was different. In the time between the journey to the hospital with Vanessa and the journey from the hospital with Vanessa and Amanda, a change had taken place which was irreversible, incredible and as profound as an experience could ever be.

It didn't seem possible that a little creature no heavier than a bowling ball had the ability to cleave life into such a clearly defined before and after. Any other vaguely comparable event would be reversible – marriage, a new job, a new home, emigrating to a different country. All of those could be done and then undone, with varying degrees of fallout. But having a child was an entirely different proposition. The bond between a parent and child could never be. It was fixed in eternity.

The same, yet different. Forever.

Nathaniel looked back at the cleaner, then at the distinct border on the floor between the clean side and the dirty side. It was the same floor, but one side was the other's opposite. It was all very binary. With some things there is no in-between. Clean or dirty. Before and after.

Alive or dead.

Sitting in that hospital cafeteria, he'd had no idea what awaited him. He'd learned quickly though. Having a child is everything everybody says it is, but amplified by a thousand. However tiring a new parent thinks it will be, multiply it by a thousand. However fun, and rewarding, and lovely, and terrifying, and relentless, and stressful and amazing it'll be to hear them say 'Mummy' or 'Daddy', multiply it all by a thousand. A million, in fact.

Parenting was everything he thought it would be, but dialled up to maximum. It was both much better and much harder than he'd imagined – but the highs outweighed the lows every day of the week. The competition was never even close.

He'd never wanted to be one of those parents who bored strangers with photos and video clips and rambling stories about random noises which may or may not have been attempts at words. But, like all parents, that's what he'd become.

He suddenly felt the urge to call Amanda, wanting to tell her he loved her and she was everything to him. That everybody loved her, and "why does everybody love Miss Amanda? Because Miss Amanda is lovely."

He smiled. She always acted like that was the corniest line in the world – and maybe it was – but he loved saying it, and he knew she loved hearing it. Putting a smile on the face of your child is an addiction, pure and simple.

He resisted the urge to call. Given that it was close to midnight he didn't think it would be particularly well-received, by either his daughter or his ex-wife.

He paused, his fork midway between his plate and his mouth.

Not ex-wife. Wife.

They were still married. Vanessa was his wife.

Why had he thought of her as an ex? They were separated, not divorced, and even that was temporary.

Although he wondered about that. Vanessa had said she needed some time, but didn't specify how much. How long is temporary before it stumbles over into permanence?

He couldn't afford to dwell on this now. He had to stay focused on his purpose.

His mission.

Chapter 13

He finished off the fish pie and forced down the rest of the cola. His wrist inexplicably felt slightly better, although he suspected that was more psychological than anything else. Unless the fish had some kind of mystical healing properties, it was probably all in his head.

Although to an extent, that was surely true of everyone and everything.

"Now you look like a man with the weight of the world on his shoulders."

Nathaniel turned to see a man wearing both a grey suit and a smile turned up to a hundred. He had a babyface so it was difficult to determine a precise age, but he somehow seemed too young to be wearing such formal attire.

"Sorry?" Nathaniel asked.

"You look concerned, brother. Are you OK?"

"Sorry, do I know... Do we know each other?"

"In some ways, everyone knows everyone, if you see what I mean. But if you mean specifically, then I don't think so. My name is Gary."

He held out his hand, which Nathaniel cautiously shook. He noticed the man's hands were almost unnaturally soft, and his nails had been manicured to within an inch of their lives.

Appearances were obviously important to this man. The question was, why?

"You look confused now, brother."

Nathaniel hesitated. He wasn't sure how to respond, or whether it was even necessary.

"Do you… work here?"

"We all work here. We've all got our purposes, don't you think?"

He smiled again, although this time it didn't quite reach his eyes.

The mention of the word *purposes*, coupled with the man's slightly unnatural appearance, made Nathaniel start to wonder if this was a real interaction or something that Aurora was showing him. He didn't remember her ever showing him anything without warning him first, or without at least making her presence known before transporting him somewhere else. And this wasn't the kind of thing she'd normally do. What would be the point in showing him an odd-looking man in the present, rather than, say, something that was going to happen in the future?

Although, if Einstein's theory about time was true, then maybe the present and the future weren't all that different anyway?

But no, this didn't feel like Aurora. Although that realisation raised more questions than it answered.

"I'm not sure if you've got me confused with someone else," Nathaniel continued. "I'm having trouble following."

"I know, brother," the man – Gary – said, taking the seat opposite Nathaniel. "Let me ask you something. It will sound strange, but bear with me. Are you familiar with quantum theory?"

"Quantum theory?" He thought of Aurora again and her explanation about dimensions and how the laws of physics could give rise to different dimensions in different places. Maybe this was a hallucination after all, or some kind of glimpse into another timeline that Aurora wanted to show him.

"Do you…" Nathaniel began, faltering slightly as he felt unsure about asking the question. "You don't know Aurora, do you?"

The man shook his head.

"I can't say I know an Aurora, brother. I've heard of the aurora borealis, but that's about it!"

Nathaniel nodded. His confusion turned to irritation now. He was getting the same feeling he got from sales reps who cold-called him at work.

"OK, Gary. What are we talking about here?"

Gary held up a hand in a conciliatory gesture.

"I know, I know. Who is this strange man talking to me in this dive? I get it. I was in your place not that long ago. Let me get to the point. Quantum systems. Did you know that quantum systems aren't actually 'real' until someone observes them? So basically nothing exists unless or until it's observed. Even colours don't exist, not as colour anyway. They exist as wavelengths, they only 'become' colours when we look at them and our brains interpret them and decide they're colours."

Nathaniel sighed.

"No offence, Gary, but it's very late at night and… as you said, we're in this service station and I'm not sure who you are or why you're telling me this."

Gary nodded as though he perfectly understood everything. He reached into his jacket and retrieved a small business card. He put it on the table and slid it over to Nathaniel.

Nathaniel read the gold font, then ran his finger across the raised lettering. Having worked at an office supply company for so long, he recognised the paper was of extremely high quality. Whoever Gary was, not only were appearances important to him, it looked like he may have the money to back them up.

But, again, who was he and why was he even talking to Nathaniel?

He read the card again, taking it in properly this time.

Dr Gareth Anderson, Director of Research.

There was no company name, just a telephone number and tagline.

Anderson has the answer. Just ask the question.

"You're a doctor?" Nathaniel asked, unable to keep the scepticism out of his voice.

"In a sense. My doctorate was in the field of parapsychology. That's where I started my project."

"Which project is that?"

"Ah. That is my baby. We are looking at the nature of reality. Myself and my team conduct experiments to determine certain things."

"What kind of things?"

"The big things. Do we live in a simulation? What is dark matter? How can we harness dark energy? Can we harness it at all? In short, the fundamental questions about the universe and our place in it as creatures made out of stardust itself."

Nathaniel still had no idea why this man was talking to him. He didn't seem like some kind of crazy loner, in fact, he was coming across more and more like some kind of salesman than anything else. An eccentric one, granted, but a salesman nonetheless.

That or a fanatical cult member looking for new recruits.

"I can see that you're not convinced, brother. Do you think we're alien-chasers? UFO-hunters? Our heads so far into our delusions that we've lost the thread of reality?"

Nathaniel thought of his own mission – he wasn't in a position to laugh at anybody else's beliefs. Not that he would ordinarily have laughed, it was more likely he'd walk away.

He was still curious as to what the man actually *wanted.*

"No," he said, "I don't think any of those things. This area just isn't something that I'm familiar with, that's all."

"I understand."

The man paused as if thinking of the best way to formulate what he wanted to say.

"Put it this way, brother," he continued, "nothing – *nothing* – exists until it is observed. That's our starting point here. There is no 'out there' until we look at it. So, where is everything before that point? And what does that say about us? Do we only exist because we 'see' ourselves? Or do we not exist at all unless *someone else* is looking at us? And if so, where are we the rest of the time? What happens when we sleep? We usually think we *go* to sleep, but maybe the truth is that because nobody is looking at us we disappear. We drift into some other realm. And who controls all this? Who switches the lights on and off for everything? For everyone? These are fundamental questions, brother. Why is nobody investigating them?"

Nathaniel thought about Aurora. Other realms could well exist – he knew that more than most. Although that did make him wonder just where Aurora went when she wasn't with him.

"Are you religious, brother?"

Nathaniel hesitated. He'd never been particularly religious, but he'd always sensed that there was more to the world than just the physical. His current situation was surely evidence of that. He'd loved, he'd hated, he'd laughed, he'd cried. How could anybody who'd done any of those things think all there is to life is material? That the universe is nothing but random atoms crashing around, creating planets, black holes, human sentience…

"I'm religious in a sense. I think."

The man smiled, and this time the smile *did* reach his eyes.

"That's good. It means we have something to work with. So in what sense are you religious? What makes you think there's something more?"

Nathaniel thought for a moment before answering. He wanted to properly consider why he felt the way he did.

"I mean, there have been countless stories through time where people have experienced supernatural or religious experiences. Some people have seen dead relatives, or have had premonitions that have come true, or... I don't know, but basically there are other paranormal and 'impossible' happenings. Surely they can't all be fake? Even if only two of those millions of experiences turn out to be true, then that's enough to prove there is more than this. And that there's... some kind of *meaning* to it all. If all that exists is what we see, and touch, and hear, then what's the point? Everything will eventually fade away into nothingness. Love wouldn't matter, neither would hate, or any other emotion."

Nathaniel thought of the despair he'd seen on the faces of the parents of the bombing victims. How could that pain, that *love* be meaningless? How could it not matter? It would mean that the parents themselves – and the children – simply didn't matter.

"You're right," the man said. "Exactly right. If this is all random, then the brain and every emotion it created would decay and dissipate into nothingness, as if they never existed in the first place. Which leads us to one of those fundamental questions, brother. To what end? Why set up a universe governed by rules and laws, only to allow it to die and for none of it to have been of any consequence?"

Nathaniel found himself warming to Gary and, in spite of the time and the location, actually enjoying the conversation.

"Yes, it wouldn't make sense. There has to be meaning behind all of this. And not just meaning that we create for ourselves, but an actual objective, outside-of-ourselves *point* to everything. Otherwise, what are we all doing here? It can't all be some cosmic accident, a mindless process going through the motions until it somehow created life."

Gary nodded as Nathaniel spoke.

"Well, we've conducted all sorts of experiments and found that processes do seem to account for a lot. The problem – for me at least – is *information*. There are scientific principles being adhered to – how did they come about? The big bang may have started the universe, but *where did the information come from to determine how that process would unfold?*

And that's before we even start to ask where the matter came from in the first place."

Nathaniel frowned. That wasn't something that had ever occurred to him, although he felt like it should have. He was comfortable with order, routine, *processes*. It had never once occurred to him that all of those things need someone to put them in place and start them off. He wasn't sure if he believed in God, but surely someone or something had to be behind it all.

If nearly four billion years ago all the matter in the universe was concentrated into a single, minute point, then who or what decreed when and how that point would begin to expand?

A thought occurred to him.

"Wait," he said, "where does this fit in with what you said about quantum systems? If nobody was observing the beginning of the universe, then how could it possibly have occurred?"

The man chuckled, then reached forward and gave Nathaniel a playful pat on the shoulder.

"Yes! Exactly!"

Nathaniel looked back at the cleaner, wondering whether he would exist if Nathaniel looked away. Surely he would – although it was a totally unprovable notion. The only way to see if he still existed would be to look, but then he would exist again.

Was that even how it worked?

As if sensing he was being looked at, the cleaner glanced over and Nathaniel realised he had been staring. He gave a sheepish smile, but the cleaner didn't reciprocate. He went back to his duties, and Nathaniel turned back to his new friend.

A throbbing started behind Nathaniel's eyes and he felt the beginnings of a headache.

"Sorry, Gary, this is very interesting, it genuinely is, but I'm very tired and—"

"Frying your brain? I understand. I'll get to the point. These experiments we do, they don't come cheap. How would you feel about sponsoring us so we can get deeper and find out the answers to some of these questions?"

Nathaniel felt himself disengage instantly.

"Sponsor you?"

"Yes, not a lot of money, don't worry we have other sponsors too. It's just that we could always use more."

It made sense now. The slick smile, the approach at a service station, the sales patter. Nathaniel had been right on both counts – the man was a salesman *and* a fanatic.

He shook his head.

"I can't sponsor you, Gary. It's been an interesting talk, but I'm not in a position to—"

"Just think about it, brother. Keep my card. We all have our purposes, brother. Maybe part of yours is to help us out – help humanity out – with these questions."

Nathaniel almost chuckled. After all he'd been through, he was pretty sure that his purpose was bigger than sponsoring a stranger to do experiments. And there was no proof Gary even was who he said he was. Yes, the business card was expensive to produce and the conversation was interesting, but what did that prove?

"Gary," he said," you're right. I do have a purpose. But this isn't it. Now if you'll excuse me, I have to get back to it."

Nathaniel wiped his hands with a napkin and began putting his empty plate and cutlery onto his tray. His hand had stopped feeling better.

"But... you can make a real difference here, brother! What's more important than finding out these answers? You'll be helping humanity."

"The thing is," Nathaniel said as he stood up. "I already am."

Chapter 14

Nathaniel threw his rubbish into the bin and stacked his tray in the shelf above, not bothering to look back at Gary. He felt slightly deflated and almost disappointed in himself for being taken in. He'd actually enjoyed the conversation. It was thought-provoking, and he felt he was on the cusp of understanding more about Aurora. He just wished there hadn't been an ulterior motive running beneath it.

He walked out of the food court, wondering briefly if he'd have made such an effort to tidy up if the cleaner wasn't around.

Was that evidence for the notion that people only do things when other people were watching?

He wasn't sure, and certainly wasn't about to go back to Gary and ask. He had work to do. He had a purpose.

The first two targets were gone. There was only one left, and he needed to get this right. If what Aurora had said was true, and the lives of countless children – not to mention their poor families – hung in the balance, then he needed to be focused.

He suddenly wondered if he would sound to the rest of the world how Gary had sounded to him.

He got into the car and rebooted the satellite navigation. He was around halfway to Birmingham at this point, which was good, although he wanted to avoid the main roads as much as possible, so wasn't sure how long the rest of the route would take. He trusted Aurora, and if there was trouble she would let him know, but his emotions still got the better of him and he still felt too exposed on the motorway. Especially so late at night and with his car headlights on – he may as well have a flashing neon sign on the roof. Drawing attention to himself, declaring his presence to all around.

It wasn't true of course, and there didn't seem to be any reason to think anybody even knew about either of the first two *bodies* yet, but he couldn't afford to take a chance. The children he was saving certainly couldn't, and if he got stopped before getting to Jonathan Owens then from what Aurora had said they would still be in danger. That still didn't make sense to him, but it's what Aurora had said. Why would she get everything else right then be wrong about this? He had to trust her. Nobody ever said having faith was easy.

As the satellite navigation system calculated the best route, he sat and wondered about the hatred a person must feel in their heart to destroy innocent lives. What would possess anyone – let alone *three* of them – to go out and kill children? To plan and scheme and prepare for mass murder? Going to work, going out to the shops, living life, and all while spending countless hours and untold energy plotting the destruction of lives. It was a frame of mind he didn't ever want to understand.

The hotel was forty-five minutes away, which meant he would arrive there at around half past midnight. Ordinarily, the timing would make him look conspicuous, although the hotel was hosting a conference for his company, which meant delegates would be arriving from all over the world at all hours of the day and night. His own arrival at that time wouldn't cause anybody to look twice.

The satellite navigation system pinged, then gave him his first instruction. In a sequence of moves that would have made Pavlov proud, he unthinkingly followed the voice and did what it told him, smoothly navigating the car park and pulling out onto the correct road. He suddenly saw the parallel with Aurora. He followed her voice, did what she told him, and trusted she'd get him where he needed to go.

He supposed faith was faith, no matter the stakes.

Inexplicably, his mind suddenly went to Vanessa, and he wondered what his wife – not *ex-wife* – was doing.

He realised that he missed both her and Amanda – albeit in different ways.

He flicked on the radio and tried to find a talk show to listen to. He didn't want music, he wanted conversation. Human beings talking to each other, interacting with each other. He needed company. Preferably without the ulterior motive of being sold to.

"...isn't the only thing that's wrong, either," a voice suddenly blared from the radio. It was the voice of an older woman, she sounded strict, like a cartoon headmistress. "I'll tell you what else is wrong, the immigrants. I'm not being racist, but if they—"

Nathaniel snapped off the radio. He'd found the surest way to know a person was about to be racist was for them to preface whatever point they were going to make with a statement about how non-racist they were about to be. It reminded Nathaniel of all the times he'd heard a person say "No offence, but," and then be incredibly offensive.

He started trying to tune another station but found it difficult to find anything other than static. Given how deep he was into what looked like a country road, that shouldn't have surprised him.

A sharp pain shot through his arm again as the pain returned. It felt as though an electric current had passed through the bone. He took his hand off the wheel and grabbed his wrist with the other hand, briefly relinquishing any control of the car. Half a second later – at most – he saw a flash at the windscreen and heard a dull thump. All at the same time he grabbed the steering wheel, slammed on the brakes, saw something tumbling ahead of him in the road, and registered a high pitched squeal coming from outside the car. He sat in the stationary car, staring into the blackness and not daring to breathe. His heart was beating too fast and he felt every muscle in his body was tense.

A thought slithered into his mind, wriggling in under the radio.

Had he hit a person?

He pushed up his mental defences and threw the thought out of his mind.

It was an animal, surely. A person wouldn't squeal, would they? If he'd hit a person then the windscreen would be cracked, and it looked fine.

So why did he feel as though the entire house of cards had crashed around him?

His hand trembling, he flicked on his full beam headlights and squinted, barely making out the outline of something in the road. It was too small to be a person. Although whatever he had hit had tumbled down the lane – so maybe it was a person, just far away?

A pain shot through his arm again, but he pushed it out of his thoughts.

The thing in the road – another *body*? – moved.

A twitch at first, then Nathaniel saw the outline of a small animal – probably a fox – try to stand and stagger pathetically on what looked like three broken legs. Nathaniel's stomach once again became a knotted rope and he felt the fish pie being squeezed up towards his throat.

He undid his seatbelt – his hand still trembling – and pushed open the car door. He was vaguely aware of a pain in his wrist, but it felt almost theoretical at this point.

He began walking cautiously towards the fox. Each time he took a step towards the flailing, wounded animal, it gave a hoarse squeal and a pathetic attempt to flee. Nathaniel wasn't close enough to see the fear in its eyes but he didn't need to be. The unmistakable aura of terror surrounded the animal like a burial shroud.

Nathaniel turned to get closer but the fox wouldn't let him get near – using what was left of its energy to jab a floppy, broken paw in Nathaniel's general direction. The high pitched, then hoarse squeal he had heard was no more; all the fox could muster now was a pathetic whimper and breathless groan each time it exerted any energy. Blood dribbled out from the right side of the animal's torso, and it was clear that the small creature couldn't possibly survive.

Nathaniel crouched down and slowly inched closer to the fox. He wanted to explain that it was an accident, that he was a good man.

"Here," he said soothingly, "it's alright. You're going to be alright."

At first the fox tried to back away again, then as if somehow realising it wasn't able to move anywhere, it relented. Nathaniel got closer and closer still, eventually reaching out a hand. The animal once again tried to back away but hardly tried at all, it'd possibly lost so much blood that it was too weak to protest anymore. Either that, or it knew death was close and wanted a last comforting touch.

Nathaniel cupped its head in his hand and the animal leaned into the warm palm. Nathaniel lightly stroked its forehead. The animal's breathing got slower, but it felt to Nathaniel that it was almost as if the fox was becoming calmer rather than not being able to breathe.

The fox looked up at Nathaniel and as he looked into the animal's eyes, his throat tightened as if a snake had wrapped around it.

He recognised the eyes.

For the briefest second, he had seen some resemblance of both men he had shot, in its pleading eyes. He couldn't pinpoint how exactly, but some twisted hybrid of both men stared out of the fox directly at him.

He fought against his instincts to run back to the car so as to soothe the poor animal. He was responsible for the fox's imminent death, surely he couldn't just walk away because *he* was uncomfortable?

The animal closed its eyes, the breathing becoming even slower but less regular now. Nathaniel continued stroking its head.

The animal's breathing suddenly cycled down into almost a whisper, each exhalation a short, warm puff of air onto Nathaniel's hand. In what must have been less than a minute, the breathing ceased altogether. The little body went limp, and Nathaniel felt the muscles under the thick coat relaxing. Never to be used or tensed again.

Chapter 15

Nathaniel looked down at the dead fox, and felt like a murderer. Not a killer, not a person trying to save others, not a soldier in a war trying to prevent an atrocity. No, a murderer.

It was a curious feeling. At first, it was almost matter-of-fact. He felt like a murderer. Simple. No judgement, no emotions attached, it just *was*. But the feeling morphed quickly, spreading and multiplying like bacteria in a petri dish. It went from a quiet sense of a new form of events to an overwhelming cacophony of noise, blasted at him and directed solely at him. He was a *murderer* with all that the word entailed and every negative emotion associated with it. There was no mitigation, no reason, no excuse. He had murdered in cold blood. The gravity of the line he'd crossed pulled him down as though into the core of the very earth.

He began weeping, then crying, then *wailing* over the animal. His own whimpers and groans mimicking the ones he'd just heard coming from the poor fox.

He kept his head down, wishing he could undo all that he'd just done. He shouldn't have taken his hand off the wheel. What was he *thinking*?

The tears streamed down his face and landed on his blood-stained hands, creating tiny, clean rivulets against the crimson red. His tears fell on the animal's thick coat, but did nothing to wash away the blood there.

Almost instinctively, he pulled the animal close to himself, embracing it and cradling its head. As if by the sheer force of willing it to be so, he could somehow make everything better.

He thought of Amanda. What kind of father was he? He couldn't even protect a defenceless animal from *himself*, let alone protect his daughter from the evil in this world.

He'd been playing with his radio, took his hand off the wheel because his wrist hurt a bit, and killed a defenceless animal. A mistake, yes, but one which was totally avoidable.

And, as such, unjustifiable.

Who had he become? What had he become?

"Murderer!" he suddenly heard himself say. "I'm nothing but a murdere—"

He stopped short as he felt the unmistakable presence of Aurora. There was no noise announcing she had arrived, no flash of light or other visual clue, he just knew she was there. The air felt different when she was around. It made him feel peaceful. Comforted.

"I did this, Aurora," he said, hearing the sadness in his own voice. "Look at what I did."

"Nathaniel," she said soothingly. "It was an accident."

"It shouldn't have happened! I should've been careful!"

"Nathaniel. It's alright."

"No! It isn't alright, Aurora. Nothing is alright. I can't go back from this! I'm a murderer. You can say it was an accident, you can say that I'm doing it to help those children, but from the outside what's the difference?"

"Nathaniel, this is nothing like—"

"It's exactly like it! What you're making me do! It's exactly the same! It's…"

He broke down then, sobbing and wailing over the body of the dead animal. For the first time he could remember – maybe the first time ever – Aurora wasn't making it better.

His mind flashed back to Gary at the service station. What objective, rational difference was there between Gary's monologues about quantum theory and his own justification for what he was doing? None. He was personally convinced by Aurora, but to the rest of the world, what good was that?

"What if none of this is real, Aurora? What if you're not?! Am I even real at this point?!"

"Nathaniel," she said quietly. "I'm sorry to have to do this."

Confused for a moment, he looked up in time to see her hand come to rest on his head, and suddenly, inexplicably, he wasn't on the road anymore.

There were trees and grass around, but this wasn't where he had been mere seconds ago. The air was still and the sun shone. The dark night had become a bright autumn day. He cautiously rose from his crouched position and looked around.

"Aurora?" he called into the ether.

He looked around but couldn't see her. He couldn't *feel* her either.

"Aurora?" he tried again, shouting this time.

He heard nothing but his own voice echoing away, ricocheting into the trees and beyond. A breeze blew through the leaves, whipping his words away with it.

He wondered exactly where he was, and if anybody or anything had heard what he had said.

If nobody heard them, had they ever even existed...?

His face felt clammy and, bringing a hand up to his cheek, he realised his tears had not yet dried. He began to wipe his eyes with the back of his hand before remembering they were covered in fox's blood. He jerked his hand away and stared at his hands. No blood. His hands were clean.

The tears hadn't dried but the blood had gone.

When had that happened? *How?*

He walked along carefully, wondering where Aurora had transported him. The breeze blew through again, this time not taking his voice away but bringing another one with it. It spoke in a calm, measured tone. It was an authoritative voice — a teacher addressing a class maybe, or a politician giving a speech.

A stern father speaking to his children?

He walked up to the edge of the thick trees, the collective age of them probably numbering into the thousands. He made his way through, weaving in- between the aged trunks.

As he walked the voice got louder and clearer, although there was still no visible sign as to where it was coming from.

Something felt amiss, but he couldn't quite place what it was. He remembered reading about the survivor of a tsunami who had felt a stillness, almost a deep peace before the incident had occurred. He wondered if that's what this was.

The calm before the storm.

He walked on, the years of fallen leaves having turned to mulch squelching and crunching underfoot. The sense that something wasn't quite right needled at him. It was like an itch he couldn't quite reach, a word he couldn't find.

He looked up at the towering trees looming overhead, and suddenly realised.

There was no birdsong. He was in a forest, surrounded by trees and shrubs and bushes. Where were the birds? How could there not be any creatures here?

Was this what the world would look like centuries after a nuclear war, when the vegetation had taken over and all other life was gone?

And, following his conversation with Gary – which now felt like an eternity ago – if that scenario ever were to actually happen, would anything even *exist* anymore if there was nobody and nothing there to see it?

As if on cue, he suddenly heard the voice again, reminding him that there were people around. Or at least one other person.

He tried to locate the source of it, heading towards it like a sailor to the Sirens.

He seemed to be heading in the right direction, as the noise was getting louder and clearer. The only sounds were the voice, the occasional rustle of leaves as the wind blew through the trees, and his shoes swishing against the undergrowth and crunching the mulch. Other than that, absolutely nothing.

He stopped.

There had been another sound, he was sure of it.

He paused, straining to identify the sound.

Definitely a noise.

Not from the same place as the voice though, it was coming from behind him. A muffled noise, as if a person was coughing into a handkerchief.

No, not coughing, *crying*.

He swung round and found himself suddenly standing in a green clearing. The trees had disappeared and he was in yet another new location.

In front of him were rows and rows of small stone monuments of varying shapes, sizes and designs. Etched into each of them were names, dates, poems, and loving inscriptions.

He knew exactly where he was.

His gaze followed each gravestone until he reached a small gathering in the centre. Each person clad in black, with a central figure – the priest – speaking to the congregation.

The authoritative tone. The sound of crying. He understood.

He heard the muffled cry again, and saw a frail lady racked with sobs. Standing next to her was the man that Aurora had previously shown Nathaniel. That time, he had worn a grey suit as he sat in his office and was told his daughter had died. This time, his entire outfit was black. His face was hollow, as though he had aged a hundred years since the last time Nathaniel had seen him. In some ways, he likely had.

The man stared down into the grave, one hand holding tightly onto his wife's waist. Next to them both stood a small boy, wearing a black suit and the look of an adult who had seen too much. The thousand yard stare of the soldier, plastered onto the face of a young innocent. No longer an innocent though. Never to be again.

It was clear to Nathaniel what Aurora was showing him. The funeral of one of the victims, the broken faces of the mourners, the decimated remnants of what used to be a whole family.

The priest finished speaking and gestured to the man Nathaniel had seen to come over.

He solemnly took the few steps to where the priest was standing and took out a folded piece of crisp white paper.

"My daughter loved a TV programme called *Play With Us*. This is the end song that they played at the finish of each programme, and I think the words are apt here. I'd like to read it to you."

Nathaniel braced himself. Amanda loved that programme, and he knew the lyrics to each song by heart. He closed his eyes, not wanting to watch. Once again, he felt the urge to run away, but felt a responsibility – a compulsion – to stay.

He felt Aurora's gentle hands on his face. The first time she'd made her presence known.

"Open your eyes, Nathaniel", she said gently, "it's important you see. This is why we're here."

The man began reciting the song lyrics that Nathaniel already had burned into his memory.

"Goodbye my friends, my lovely friends, I've had a lovely day. Goodbye my friends, my lovely friends, it's been fun to laugh and play. Goodbye my friends, my lovely friends, I'm feeling over the moon. Goodbye my friends, my lovely friends—"

The man's voice broke at the next line, the tears that had welled up in his eyes bursting forth and streaming down his pained face.

"I hope… to see you soon."

The man kept his head down as his shoulders spasmed as if absorbing the force of his sobs. His trembling hands refolded the paper and put it back into his pocket.

He shuffled back to where his wife and son stood, the broken family weeping with and hugging each other. Not for the first time, Nathaniel thought, and not for the last.

The man suddenly looked up, his eyes locking onto Nathaniel's. The atmosphere changed, charged with an electricity Nathaniel had never experienced before. There was almost an audible hum in the air.

"You can stop this," the man whispered, his words somehow reaching Nathaniel although apparently not heard by anybody else. "You are the only one who can stop this. Keep going, Nathaniel. Save my little girl. Save our family."

As the man spoke, Nathaniel felt the back of his neck burn. He sensed that it had turned red, as though burnt by the sun. He realised that's how it felt looking into the man's eyes – it was like staring at the sun. An elemental force, ferociously burning for billions of years, trained on

him and him alone. But there was an undercurrent to it —
not powerful but *powerless*. A pleading.

Was Nathaniel really the only person who could
prevent the sun from going out? If Aurora was to be
believed — and why wouldn't she? — then it looked like it.

He opened his mouth to respond, but found he
couldn't speak. The mourners had frozen too. The family,
the priest, the friends and relatives — paralysed.

A thought occurred to him then, as he stared at the
tableau. Mentally noting who was there to pay their respects,
he realised that none of the little girl's friends were there. If
a school-aged little girl had died, where were all her—

"They died too, son," the priest said solemnly. He
slowly broke from whatever paralysis was inflicting the rest
of the mourners, and looked up at Nathaniel. His gaze was
no less forceful than the man's had been. His voice again
somehow a whisper yet totally clear to Nathaniel across the
expanse of the cemetery.

"They were a group of four little girls," he
continued. "They'd known each other since they had met at
nursery. They're all gone now, son. All of them. They're
with Amanda now."

Nathaniel felt a detonation in his soul. Any trace of
doubt or fear fled from his mind — as if terrified of their
host's determination.

In an instant he was back in reality, standing by his car looking down at the fox.

"Nathaniel," Aurora said gently, "everyone who has faith in anything will have periods of doubt. It comes with the territory. Just remember, no amount of doubt can make something untrue."

"And no amount of faith can make something true, either," he said quietly.

"You're right, Nathaniel. That is very true. The difference is that you've seen the truth, you've felt it. Please don't allow doubts to sway you from your purpose. You're so close, Nathaniel."

He looked into her face and knew she was right. He had seen the results of his own inaction, he knew what was in store if he failed in this.

He knew what would happen to Amanda.

"Are you ready, Nathaniel?" Aurora asked him calmly.

"I am ready, Aurora," he said defiantly. "I have to stop this."

Chapter 16

The rest of the journey went by in what felt like mere minutes.

Someone had once told Nathaniel that after a certain amount of time, driving becomes an unconscious activity, rather than a conscious one. It becomes automatic. People don't need to think about what they're doing anymore, they just do it on autopilot while their minds drift somewhere else. That's why a person can drive an entire car journey and not remember any of it. Unless something notable happens – like hitting a fox, for example – the driver generally has no specific recollection of anything that happened en route.

That's how Nathaniel felt as he stepped out of his car in the hotel car park. His mind had been solidly on his mission, and nothing else.

Considering he'd stopped on the way, after hitting the fox and then going... wherever it was Aurora had taken him, he had made pretty good time. He had hoped to arrive at the hotel at around half past midnight, but after all that it was closer to one o'clock. He'd pulled over once more about ten minutes from the hotel after realising his clothes were covered in blood, and had hastily got changed while parked in a lay-by. He had crawled into the back seat so as not to look too conspicuous. A grown man changing out of bloody clothes at the side of the road in the early hours of the morning wasn't a good look for anyone.

The conference was due to last the entire weekend, and Nathaniel knew that Jonathan Owens, his third and final target, would be attending. They weren't friends, but they'd met a couple of times and traded emails around company business here and there. Jonathan would know Nathaniel – probably more by name than by face – so he shouldn't have a problem getting close to him. Close enough to do what he needed to do, anyway.

Aurora had given him an outline again. He would phone Owens and arrange to meet him in his hotel room for a brief chat about something work related. It couldn't be about anything too urgent, but at the same time, it had to be something that needed to be sorted out fairly soon, otherwise Owens wouldn't agree to meet. Once inside the room, it would just be a matter of time until Nathaniel got the chance to do what he needed. The whole thing should only take a matter of minutes, and Aurora had told Nathaniel not to clean up or do much afterwards. He just needed to get in and out as soon as possible, without touching anything and preferably without being seen by anyone. After that, it would be straight back into the car and on the road to London and Amanda's school concert.

He'd booked one night at the hotel under a false name, so there would be no reason later for anybody else from the company to think he had been there. As long as he kept his head down so nobody spotted him there shouldn't be a problem.

He wondered about Owens and his personal life. Would anybody miss him over the weekend? Nathaniel didn't know if Owens was married, but he doubted it. Even if he was, and his wife tried to call him over the weekend, the fact he was busy at a conference would mean she probably wouldn't be too concerned if he didn't answer his phone.

He wondered if Owens had kids. Probably not, given what Aurora had shown him Owens was going to do. How could a father inflict that kind of damage? And if he did have children, and was going to go on and bomb other peoples' children, then his kids would be better off without him anyway. Their own lives would be better too, without having to experience the stigma and residual pain of being the children of a mass murderer.

The conference was a huge, international event – nobody would miss a man at Owens' level. He wasn't a guest speaker, he wasn't high up in the company. Just another employee in a suit as far as anybody was concerned. As much as people like to think of themselves as individuals, a group of people in suits are as anonymous as cogs in a machine.

Nathaniel took his bags from the car and made his way towards the hotel. It had a pristine, glass front, with what looked like an oak reception desk staffed by two tired-but-somehow-enthusiastic-looking staff members.

As he stepped through the automatic doors there was a low hum of chatter and socialising. Considering it was past one o'clock in the morning, it was actually very busy, although he wasn't too surprised. It was more the *excitement* that he was surprised by – surely at 1am everybody should be forgiven for just wanting to check- in and go to bed? Although if this conference was like others he'd attended, a lot of people were probably just there for the free food and the fun of staying in a hotel where they would be pampered and looked after for a couple of days. And to top it all, it wouldn't cost them a penny. In fact they'd get paid overtime for 'working' over the weekend.

A group of men and women in crumpled suits stood at the check-in desk, each person holding the obligatory wheeled suitcase with an oversized airport luggage tag on the handle. They had the classic look of weary travellers normally seen at airports – tired and dehydrated, but with a vague air of excitement surrounding them.

One of the women in the group made a joke – Nathaniel could tell by her facial expression and exaggerated body language – and two of her colleagues laughed heartily. The laughter burst into the air, seemingly ricocheting off the glass and marble. Nathaniel kept watching, and noticed that, just after making the joke, in the moments after her colleagues had laughed, the woman's face suddenly lost any trace of amusement. Her face went from beaming smile to stone-cold-sober in milliseconds. It was one of those telling gestures that gives a person away despite their best efforts. Whatever she had said, whatever joke she had made, as soon as it had served its purpose she had dropped the performance. Nathaniel stood and watched, rapt for a moment, as if given a rare glimpse into what was behind the mask. That had always fascinated him, the discrepancies between the public face and the private one.

Nathaniel was the only person who had seen her serious side in that moment. The only person who ever would. If he hadn't been standing there, if he hadn't been looking at that exact point, she still would have done it. It would have happened, but nobody would have seen it - which was as good as it not happening.

In spite of himself, he thought back to Gary, wondering why his words seemed to have burrowed so deeply into his mind. As Gary had said, if nobody witnesses something, then does it even exist? For that group of colleagues, all that existed was the woman's joke and the demeanour that she had allowed them to see. To all intents and purposes, anything else she may have been feeling or thinking may as well not have existed.

He wondered where his own current circumstances and persona fit into that.

One of the other women started talking to her then, and Nathaniel saw the woman's performance begin again. Business as usual. Everyone wore masks, Nathaniel knew that. He had his work side and his home side, just like everybody else. The rarity was being given that glimpse behind the curtain. It felt almost like catching out a person in a lie. Almost voyeuristic.

The desk clerk, having assumedly checked the group into their rooms, called Nathaniel over to the desk.

"Good morning, sir," he said more cheerfully than was strictly necessary given the time, "are you checking- in for the conference?"

Nathaniel felt his own mask effortlessly glide onto his face, as he politely explained that he wasn't aware of any conference and was just passing through on the way to visit relatives.

The man checked him in and the two of them made small talk. So much of life was a game with defined rules and roles for the participants. The clerk was to be friendly and professional, Nathaniel was to be the same but was supposed to have an air of extra relaxation or excitement about him due to the fact he was checking into a hotel. Maybe he was a frequent and bored traveller, or maybe he was a tired one, or maybe he was just another suit at a conference hoping to network and schmooze, but in any case, he had a role to play. The clerk would tell him about the room's facilities, and Nathaniel would nod and smile and at the end thank him for his help.

Then Nathaniel would shuffle off the conveyor belt, and the next person would jump on. Similarly, the next participant in Nathaniel's life would then shuffle onto his own conveyor belt. Maybe the person manning the lift, or possibly a tourist wondering why on earth the hotel was suddenly swamped with people in suits. They would all play their roles though, any deviation would cause them to be looked upon as just that – deviants. Breaking the social etiquette that has evolved over time into an art form. Daring to go against what is expected.

Nathaniel wondered how they would view him if they knew what he was doing. Although he supposed that would depend on context. To the parents of the children he was saving, right now he was nothing to them. They'd probably see him as a killer. But if their child died and they knew he could've stopped it, they'd view him as a monster. He'd be considered as bad as the bombers themselves. Worse in some ways.

That was the thing that bothered Nathaniel about the whole endeavour. The only way to prove without a shadow of a doubt that he was saving lives was to let the bombings happen. But how could he do that? What kind of person allows innocent children to be killed if they are in a position to stop it?

His reward wouldn't be public acclaim or tearful thank yous. His reward would be knowing he'd saved lives, and – more importantly than that, more important than *anything* – his reward would be his little girl. Safe. Protected.

And as long as Amanda was OK, Nathaniel would be OK. No matter how this ended.

Nathaniel got to his room, dumped his bags on the floor and lay down on the bed. He felt a tiredness that he'd never experienced before. He was psychologically, emotionally, and physically spent, all at once.

He felt the warm, soothing hands of sleep pulling him gently down into the mattress. He didn't resist.

As he drifted off, he wondered about the binary choice he was left with.

Was he a protector of the innocent? A warrior single-handedly stopping a massacre?

Or was he a deluded killer? Allowing his brain to give him a justification for committing serial murder?

And, in the end, when this was all over and the dust had settled, would the distinction even matter to anyone other than him?

Chapter 17

Nathaniel awoke in the dark with the vague sense that he had dreamed about the fox. The dream came to him in fragments over the next few minutes, and soon the entire picture soon became clear.

In the dream, he hadn't killed it at all, he had seen it in time and swerved to miss it. He yanked the steering wheel to the right, but found it locked in that position. A surge of adrenalin took over and he stomped on the brake pedal but inexplicably found it accelerated the vehicle. The last moments of his life – before he slammed into the lorry in the other lane – were spent frantically trying to shift the steering wheel.

He'd saved the fox, but killed himself.

Lying in the dark he wondered if that was his choice now, here, in reality? Was it really kill or be killed? Not that any of the three men were a threat to his life directly, although he knew that life without Amanda certainly wouldn't be a life at all. And living the rest of his life in the knowledge that he had allowed countless children to be massacred? Not a life even remotely worth living.

He'd seen the families, their grief and pain. He'd watched the schools burn. Aurora had shown him everything.

For the first time in his life, he allowed himself to wonder just what Aurora would do if he failed. Would she torment him with screams for the rest of his life? Would she keep showing him glimpses of the people he could've saved, but didn't? He didn't think she would do that, but it was a moot point anyway. Allowing children to die, watching the footage unfold on the news and recognising the faces of the innocent lives he could've saved would be punishment enough.

He checked the time and realised he'd been asleep for five hours straight. It was the longest block of sleep he'd had for a long time. Not that he felt particularly refreshed.

As if sensing a slight feeling of peace, a sudden surge of panic inexplicably rose up in him, mirroring the one he'd felt in his dream, and he was suddenly convinced that every police officer in the country was looking for him.

He fumbled around and found the remote control, clicking on the TV and flicking through channels until he found the news. A body had been found in a lake somewhere in the North, and another had been found with stab wounds in a parked car, but there was nothing about a body being found in his office or anyone being found in an apartment. There was also nothing about people going missing, although he thought it was probably too regular an occurrence to make the news. It also hadn't been that long, even though it'd felt to Nathaniel like an eternity.

It was only a matter of time before the first two bodies were found, he knew that. He just hoped he'd taken enough precautions and been careful enough so there'd be no link to him.

Although what was the alternative, even if he knew he'd eventually get caught? Even if he knew undoubtedly that at some point the police would catch up with him? He knew what the outcome would be. He'd seen it. He'd *felt* it.

History was littered with unsung heroes, he was prepared to be one of them if it meant his little girl would be safe.

He would finish this, and the chips could fall where they may.

The plan was to call Owens and somehow get into his room before breakfast. That was going to be easier said than done, but Nathaniel knew he could do it. He'd had plenty of other firsts recently, this would be merely another.

He found Owens' work mobile phone number, and dialled it from the hotel room phone. He couldn't use his own mobile for obvious reasons.

As the phone began to ring, he suddenly realised that he didn't even know if Owens had arrived yet. Maybe he was driving up for the morning registration only, or arriving later for some reason, or something had happened and he couldn't attend at all. He hadn't thought to check, even though it was a vital part of the

"Hello?" a frantic voice said through the earpiece.

"Hello, Jonathan?"

"Yes! Why didn't you text?"

"Sorry?"

There was a pause on the line. Nathaniel got the sense that the voice on the other end of the phone was just as confused as he was.

"Who is this, please?"

"Sorry, Jonathan, it's Nathaniel Bennett. Sector Eight office?"

Nathaniel could almost hear the cogs whirring in Owens' mind as he tried to place the voice and name of this stranger.

"Nathaniel? Yes. Sorry, I thought you were... Why are you... it's very early."

"I know, Jonathan, I'm sorry. I'm here at the Birmingham conference, are you?"

"Yes, I'm here. I didn't realise the Sector heads were invited this year too. I suppose that means Brian the Bore and Trudi the Tyrant are here as well, does it?"

Nathaniel gave a forced chuckle.

"I'm not sure, Jonathan, I haven't seen them. I only got here a couple of hours ago."

"I'll call Jada and find out if you like."

"No! Um… no, thanks. That's fine, Jonathan, I'm sure I'll catch up with everyone later."

"Alright. Well how can I help you, Nathaniel?"

"It's probably better to have a quick chat."

There was a pause on the line.

"I thought that's what we were doing, Nathaniel."

"No, I mean in person. Would that be alright?"

Another pause, another weary sigh.

"Fine. I'll be going down for breakfast in a while so we can meet there."

"Er… would it be OK if we met in one of our rooms instead? It's a slightly sensitive matter."

Another pause, this one longer. Nathaniel stared at the curtains, suddenly noticing that the deep red colour looked almost like bloo—

"Alright, Nathaniel, I'm in room 238. I'll be going to breakfast in around fifteen minutes, so try and get here quickly and we can… sort everything out."

"Will do, Jonathan. I'll see you in a couple of minutes."

Nathaniel hung up the phone and instantly felt as though the temperature in the room had ratcheted up. It was as though some unseen heat source had erupted into life. Whatever it was had burned the oxygen out of the place – it was stifling and hard to breathe.

The sensation didn't last long. A sudden calm overtook him, and he knew who had stepped into the room.

He looked around and saw Aurora, smiling.

"This is the last time you will ever have to do this, Nathaniel," she said kindly. "This one action will ensure the safety of so many children. And Amanda."

She was right, this would be it. Then Amanda would be safe.

He changed into the clothes he was to wear for this third target – everything had been planned in advance by Aurora, so he didn't need to think about details like that. He retrieved the gun, checked it was loaded and that the suppressor hadn't come loose, then put it in his back pocket.

"He's in Room 238," Nathaniel suddenly blurted.

Aurora smiled.

"I know, Nathaniel…"

He looked at her, and registered the kind amusement in her eyes.

"Of course you do," he said sheepishly. "I should've just asked you, not him."

"It doesn't make a difference, Nathaniel. It's all fine."

She stepped over and placed a warm hand on his shoulder.

"Nathaniel," she said, her voice echoing strangely around the room. "You can do this."

He nodded.

"Yes," he said.

"No, Nathaniel," she said, slightly sterner this time. "I'm not asking whether you can, I'm telling you that you can. You've come this far. You can do this. This is your purpose in life, like I said. You're fortunate enough to know that. Many people don't. You'll succeed, Nathaniel."

Whatever was radiating from her hand now imbued him with a determination, a strength. He didn't need to see visions of the future or speak to families of the future-deceased, he was ready. All he had to do was leave the room and follow the plan.

He double-checked his pockets, grabbed his keycard, and went to meet Jonathan Owens.

Chapter 18

Jonathan shook his head.

He hadn't received the text yet, which wasn't good news. He'd switched his phone off and then on again, just in case there'd been a problem, or some kind of glitch.

Nothing.

Where *was* he? He was supposed to get in touch last night. This wasn't like him.

Jonathan walked over and slid open the large wardrobe door. He scanned the rails and made an angry noise somewhere between a growl and a scoff.

Where was his green tie? For fuck's sake!

He'd packed it. He knew he did because he planned to wear it on the first day of the conference. So where was the stupid thing?

He pulled the suitcase out from the bottom of the wardrobe, flung it on the bed and yanked it open. He rifled through it, pushing clothes around as though punishing them for some slight.

No tie.

What was going *on* today? No text, no tie. Was nothing going to go right?!

He stood and stared at his suitcase with his hands on his hips, as though giving it a stern enough look would somehow persuade it to give him back his tie.

"Fuck it, then!" he said defiantly to some imagined audience. He'd wear the red one.

The hotel phone rang, and he snatched it up, wondering for a split second whether they'd arranged a phone call and not a text at all.

"Hello?" he said, hearing his voice sounding raspy and hoarse. Other than swearing at clothing, he hadn't spoken out loud yet today.

"Hello, Jonathan?"

At fucking last!

"Yes! Why didn't you text?"

"Sorry?"

Jonathan suddenly realised he didn't recognise the voice. So who was it, and why the fuck had he still not received that text?!

"Who is this, please?"

He listened as a colleague – although hardly one he knew very well – rambled on about wanting to meet him. He wasn't particularly interested until the man – Nathaniel something – mentioned that he wanted to talk to him about a *sensitive matter*.

Something clicked in his mind.

Maybe there wasn't to be a text at all. Was it possible Nathaniel was in on the plan now, too? Why hadn't anyone told him?

It didn't seem likely, but it made sense. No text, and suddenly this man wanted to meet at stupid o'clock in the morning to discuss a sensitive matter. What else could it be?

He suddenly realised he couldn't remember the room number, so read it off the phone.

"Alright, Nathaniel," he said, "I'm in room 238. I'll be going to breakfast in around fifteen minutes, so try and get here quickly and we can… sort everything out."

Jonathan's colleague hung up the phone.

He went to the mirror and began the almost automatic process of fastening his red tie.

He avoided his own gaze in the mirror. He'd been doing that a lot recently.

Chapter 19

Vanessa hadn't been awake long.

It was one of those nights where, even though she could see from the clock that she'd slept for six hours straight, she felt as though she'd lay down to sleep, blinked, and suddenly it was morning. She hadn't got used to sleeping or waking up alone. Not yet anyway.

It still felt strange after so many years of sharing the bed with Nathan to not have him here. Although she wasn't sure if she missed *him* being there or just missed *someone* being there. In any case there was a definite void next to her.

She lay in bed listening to Amanda downstairs.

She heard her opening and closing their creaking cupboard doors slowly, which only served to make the noise even louder. At one point she must have switched on the television without realising how loud it would be, so Vanessa heard a burst of noise which was then frantically muted.

Amanda was obviously trying to be quiet, which somehow made her even noisier than usual. At one point Vanessa heard a clatter, and pictured her young daughter frozen to the spot, on tiptoes, hoping she hadn't just woken her mum. It reminded her of her own teenage years – creeping back home at all hours, trying not to wake her parents but finding that someone had turned the volume up on the house. The stairs wouldn't creak as she'd stepped up them, so much as scream in an attempt wake up the house.

She's home late everyone, and she's been drinking too!

Not that her parents minded particularly. They'd given her a lot of freedom. Maybe too much, she thought now. Maybe so much that she didn't know how to be anything other than free. A caged animal is still in a cage, no matter how pretty or comfortable the bars may be.

Her teenage years. A lifetime ago. Before full-time work, the mortgage, Nathan.

Before motherhood.

Not that she resented being a mother – far from it. She adored carrying Amanda in her womb, loved feeling the million kicks and random hiccups. Even the heartburn was a reminder that something miraculous was happening inside her. The scariest moments of her life had been those times during the pregnancy when she'd realise she hadn't felt her baby move for a while. Then of course, she'd lie down to sleep and the baby would take that as a cue to have a party. She'd sworn Amanda would turn out to be a footballer or a boxer, based solely on the internal kicks, jabs and uppercuts she'd felt.

Motherhood was incredible, there was no doubt about it. It was just so *exhausting*. People had warned her of course. As soon as she'd got pregnant she'd heard the old classics – "Make sure you make the most of sleeping in now!" "Ooh, you'll never sleep properly again!" It was all very hilarious and not at all annoying...

What she didn't realise was that motherhood involved being exhausted, then being pushed to your limit of exhaustion where you couldn't take any more, and then being pushed even further. It was the ultimate endurance test. An entirely self-imposed one, as well as one that no participant would change for the world.

It was more complex than that, of course. She never quite knew where Vanessa the Mum ended and Vanessa the Individual began. Maybe that was part of the deal. The baby isn't the only new life that enters the world – the pre-parents become parents, with all that entails. While the baby is learning to be human, the parents are going through their own, incredibly steep, learning curve.

She remembered telling Shaye how trapped she'd felt. And it was true, but she did wonder if she'd misrepresented things somewhat. Yes, she felt trapped, but not by Nathan, and not by Amanda.

She felt trapped by herself.

Deep down she knew she could walk away. Plenty of mums and wives – and dads and husbands – make the decision to either literally or figuratively walk away from their responsibilities. But she wouldn't allow herself to do it. She'd known at the moment Amanda was born – in fact, the moment she found out she was pregnant – that she would be the best mum she could be. Amanda and Nathan weren't keeping her in her current life, her own sense of needing to be a good mother and wife was.

And what was wrong with that? So much of life is held together by a sense of duty, of obligation. Of being a good mother, father, wife, husband, daughter, son. Being a good *person*.

Yes, she could walk away, but she'd never forgive herself for the type of person that would make her.

As if on cue, she heard the faint sound of Amanda practising her piano piece for the concert later. She could tell Amanda wasn't pressing the keys full force, and was holding back so as not to make too much noise. A sense of pride rushed in and overwhelmed her, and she felt tears prick her eyes. Her daughter had got up early to practise her piano piece, and was being considerate enough not to practise too loud. On top of that, it was a piano piece that she had composed herself, no less. With her teacher's help, of course, but it was still impressive.

This was what being a parent meant. She was mentally, physically and emotionally exhausted, she'd spent untold hours wondering what else her life could be – wondering *who* else she could be – but in an instant, her daughter could make that all disappear merely by existing.

She just wished she felt the same way about her husband. His presence had become more a cause of stress than the alleviation of it. And yes, she had a duty as a wife – just as he had a duty as a husband – but that obligation felt much more flexible, much more tenuous, than the bond she felt with her child. People get divorced from their spouses all the time, but they didn't divorce their kids. It was a different bond. Both were forged in love, but only one of them felt unbreakable.

She closed her eyes and allowed the music to wash over her. She pictured Amanda at the piano, knowing she was probably slouching her shoulders slightly the way she always did. She wouldn't do that at the concert though, Vanessa knew that. She'd have perfect posture when she needed it.

Vanessa suddenly felt that familiar pang of missing her daughter even though she was in close proximity, and felt an overwhelming need to tell her how proud she was.

She got up, grabbed her dressing gown and made her way down the stairs.

She wanted to surprise her daughter with a kiss or a hug from behind, so stepped carefully. Every so often a step would creak – it was her teenage self all over again – but she made it to the bottom without Amanda seeming to notice. If she had, she certainly hadn't stopped playing.

Being this close to the piano, Vanessa suddenly realised how loud the music was, even though Amanda was trying to be quiet, and regretted the amount of wine she'd drank last night. She'd suffer a headache for her child though.

Parenting in a nutshell, she thought with a wry smile on her face.

She stood in the doorway and watched her only child playing her mostly-self-composed piece. Even though she couldn't see Amanda's face, she knew the exact facial expression she'd have. An intense look of concentration, her brow furrowed accentuating the little dimple in- between her eyes.

She watched her fingers glide over the keys, hitting every note with varying degrees of pressure. She'd been right about the shoulders too.

"Are you going to just stand there, Mum?" Amanda suddenly asked cheekily, not missing a beat and continuing to play.

Vanessa smiled.

"Well," she said, "I was going to tell you to straighten your shoulders but I thought I'd wait until you finished."

Amanda fixed her posture and gave a sheepish, "Oops!"

She was still note perfect as she adjusted her playing position, Vanessa noticed. She walked over and gave her little girl a kiss on the top of her head. The part that used to be her fontanelle.

"Morning, Mum," she said with a chuckle.

"Good morning, Miss Amanda," Vanessa said, hearing her husband's phrase inexplicably come out of her own mouth.

Amanda turned with an incredulous look on her face.

"You sound like Dad!" she said, and gave a chuckle.

Vanessa smiled but there was little humour in it. Had she started becoming like Nathan? She didn't like the thought of losing her identity and having it merge with another person's. Is that what was happening? Would she one day be content in this life not because she'd accepted it but because she'd changed – in increments, unnoticeably until it was too late? Was that the essence of marriage - two people making a million compromises to the point that they became unrecognisable from who they were?

She rubbed her eyes. It was too early for this much introspection. She'd make some coffee and start the day.

She watched Amanda play a bit longer, hoping that Nathan wouldn't disappoint her by missing the concert. Not that he was unreliable – far from it, she could set her watch by him - but she just got a sense that it might be different this time. Maybe because they lived in separate homes, or for some other reason, but something just felt slightly... off. She couldn't quite place it, she just felt that maybe Nathan wouldn't get to the concert today.

She was overthinking.

Coffee, she said to herself, and walked to the kitchen.

Chapter 20

Stepping into the hotel corridor felt like entering a soundproofed room. The deep, lush carpets and what Nathaniel assumed was thick wallpaper seemed to dampen the noise of his footsteps as he walked down the hallway to Owens' room. It was both a comforting and unnerving experience.

As Nathaniel passed hotel room doors he heard snippets of conversations, or the morning news, or a hairdryer, but in- between doors everything felt still, silent. It reminded Nathaniel of films he'd watched where a person is walking down a pitch-black street, illuminated every so often by the street lamps but then disappearing into the dark in between each one.

He wondered about that. Was he walking in the light, or in the dark?

The numbers on the doors acted like a countdown. Owens was in 238, and Nathaniel watched as the even numbers descended like a countdown. 248, 246, 244, 242, 240…

238.

He stood outside the door and listened.

There were no voices, not even the sound of a television.

He took a deep breath and subconsciously patted his pocket, ensuring the gun was where it should be.

This was it. The last stretch.

He raised his hand to knock on the door and felt the sudden, unmistakable sensation of his mobile phone vibrating in his pocket.

"Shit!" he blurted, fumbling to get to his phone. Had it been on this whole time? He swore he'd turned it off so he couldn't be tracked. How did he manage to forget to turn it off?!

He stepped away from Owens' door and retrieved his phone. By the time he got to it, it had stopped. He looked at the call log and saw it had been Vanessa who was calling.

Why was Vanessa calling this early? A pang of anxiety shot through his already-heightened body.

"Nathaniel," Aurora said out of the ether. "We're running out of time."

"I know," he blurted. "Just... one minute. Maybe something's happened to Amanda."

"It hasn't, Nathaniel," Aurora said kindly, but with a tone of urgency in her voice. "They're both fine. We don't have time. He's going to be leaving soon."

He looked over at Aurora, who had materialised in the hallway now. He trusted her – of course he did, look at where he was and what he was doing – but he still couldn't shake the sense that something was wrong. Maybe it was panic, or maybe he simply wanted to prolong meeting Owens, but he felt compelled to call.

"I have to," he said, "I have to make sure they're OK. I can't do this otherwise."

He tapped the call button on the screen and held the phone to his ear, his eyes fixed on Aurora. He hoped she was right – and knew somewhere in his mind that she was – but he just wanted to hear Vanessa's voice. Or Amanda's voice. Maybe hearing her would strengthen his resolve. He didn't know, but he needed something.

The phone rang out.

He felt his expression change from concern to panic.

"They're OK, Nathaniel. I promise."

He shook his head. Something was wrong.

He redialled, holding the phone to his ear and gripping it with knuckles which were rapidly turning white.

On the fourth ring Vanessa answered.

"Hello, Nathan."

"Vanessa!" he blurted, hearing the desperation in his own voice. "Are you OK?"

"I'm fine, Nathan, I just wanted to check you're still coming today."

He rolled his eyes and felt both relief and annoyance wash over him.

"Of course I'm still coming toda— Vanessa, do you genuinely believe I'd miss it? Is that why you called?"

"I don't know, Nathan. I just wanted to make sure."

"Well… don't! I said I'll be there, Vanessa. Why wouldn't I come to my own daught—"

"Hi, Dad!" he heard Amanda call out from somewhere.

"Miss Amanda!" he said, "are you OK, princess? Are you all ready for today?"

He heard a rustling sound as Vanessa handed the phone to Amanda.

"I think so," she said, "I've been practising enough!"

"I know, princess. And I'm very proud of you."

"Thanks, Dad. It'll be worth it. Like you always say, nothing good ever comes without a struggle."

He looked over at Aurora.

"I know, princess," he said softly. "I know. The struggle is part of the process, isn't it?"

"That's what you keep telling me so it must be!"

He smiled.

"See you later, Dad! Love you!"

"I love you too, Miss Amanda. I love you so much."

Vanessa came back on the line.

"I just want to make sure you'll be there, Nathan. I've just been feeling... never mind."

"I'll be there," he said, his eyes still on Aurora. "I won't miss it. Now, I have to go."

He hung up the phone, and slipped it back in his pocket. A determination of molten iron coursed through his veins and he felt a certainty that he would get his family back. Vanessa would change her mind once she knew what he'd done for them. Once she realised the risks he'd taken and the sacrifices he'd made to save Amanda. Any man who would do what he was doing to save his daughter – not to mention the countless other children he was saving – would surely be forgiven everything else. Aurora had shown him the carnage that would be wreaked if he didn't. He was preventing the annihilation of countless innocent lives. Mass slaughter on an almost unimaginable scale. Except he didn't need to imagine it, Aurora had shown him. He'd seen the bodies – the ones impacted by the initial blasts and the ones injured with shrapnel. He'd heard the explosions, and the screams, and the wails of the arriving parents. He'd smelled the acrid, nightmarish stench of burning timber and metal and plastics and bodies. The separate aromas mixing in the air, twisting and congealing into a single scent announcing one thing only. Death.

And that, after all, was what he was saving Amanda from. Their beautiful little girl. Once Vanessa knew that, she wouldn't be angry with him. How could she? Every moment of their lives shared with Amanda from this point on would be a direct result of the sacrifices Nathaniel was now making. She'd take him back, and love him more than ever.

What kind of mother would turn her back on the man who saved her child?

Feeling a renewed sense of purpose, and that determination forged in a furnace still running through his body, he stepped back in front of the door and knocked.

He patted the gun again. It was where it needed to be, it was ready.

And so was Nathaniel.

Chapter 21

Nathaniel knocked on the door, feeling his heart beating through his shirt and his adrenalin sky high. Prepared for war.

There was a slight rustling noise from inside and Nathaniel subconsciously patted the gun again. It was amazing how quickly it had gone from something he'd never even consider using – something he'd only ever seen in films – to being an almost comforting presence.

The door opened and Jonathan Owens stood in front of Nathaniel with an odd look on his face. Nathaniel tried to read the expression, but it was somewhere between confusion, curiosity and – oddly – something that looked like relief.

"Jonathan," Nathaniel said, managing to disguise the fear he was feeling. "Thank you for agreeing to see me."

He held a hand out, but Owens didn't shake it. Instead he nodded briefly, then waved a hand towards the room. Nathaniel stepped inside, noticing that Owens poked his head out of the door as if making sure nobody else had followed.

He closed the door and turned to Nathaniel.

"So?" he asked. His expression was an expectant one now, but there was still something off about it. He didn't seem to be curious about why Nathaniel was there, it was more that he was waiting for Nathaniel to give him something that he wanted.

"Thank you again for agreeing to meet with me, Jonathan. I know it's early."

Owens nodded again.

"I don't mind that it's early," he said. "Is this about…?"

He looked expectantly at Nathaniel and waited.

Nathaniel tried to read his face again but was drawing even more of a blank than earlier.

"It's about an account we have in common, funnily enough," he continued.

"Yes?"

"Yes."

"Do we have anything else in common?"

Nathaniel hesitated and wondered if he'd walked into some sort of trap.

What could Owens possibly be talking about? They barely knew each other, what would they have in common except for work?

"Sorry, I don't… I don't follow."

Owens walked over to the table next to the bed, and began putting on an expensive-looking watch.

"I mean," he said, "is there anything you need to tell me?"

Nathaniel frowned. This wasn't going to plan. At all.

"Is there anything," Owens continued, "that, say, you were going to tell me through a text message today? Confirmation of something? A plan, maybe?"

At the mention of a plan Nathaniel felt his heart rate quicken, which he hadn't thought was even possible.

"I don't… think so."

"Oh, come on!" Owens snapped. "Do you really want me to spell it out?!"

Nathaniel's already heightened state ratcheted up a notch. He wondered whether now would be the time to pull out the gun.

"Jonathan, I'm sorry, I genuinely don't know what you're referring to."

The man's shoulders dropped and his air of welcome dissipated like smoke. He took out his phone and checked for something – a text message, Nathaniel wondered? – and then shook his head.

"So if you don't want to tell me anything about… If you aren't here to… What exactly are you here for,

Nathaniel? This can't be about the fire because nobody knows anything yet – it's all just speculation."

"Fire? What fir— No, like I said, I needed to speak with you about an account."

"Which one?"

"The Wilkinson plant. I believe you worked on that."

"The Wilkinson plant? That's... I did work on it but that's almost a year old. Why would you need to come here now and talk to me about it?"

"I was just going over some—"

Before he could finish, Owens took a step and was suddenly standing close. Too close. When he spoke his voice was gentle, almost kind.

"Nathaniel, I don't think you're here to talk about the Wilkinson plant. I think there's a message you need to give me, and it's OK. It's all OK. I'm *expecting* it, so just tell me. Are we on or are we off? That's all I need to know. Is it happening?"

Nathaniel stared at the man, hoping Aurora would arrive and let him know just what was going on. His confusion must have been evident on his face.

"Have you heard," asked Owens, "of saccadic masking?"

Nathaniel shook his head slowly.

"It's a major cause of car accidents, or at least hitting someone or something that seemed to come out of nowhere."

Nathaniel thought of the fox – the eyes boring into him - but shook the image from his head.

"In short," Owens continued, "saccadic masking is when your brain blinds you. It happens when your eyes move so that you don't end up seeing blurred images as your eyes flick from one thing to another. If our brains didn't do it, then whenever we looked from one thing to another without moving our heads we'd see blurred images that made no sense. It's very clever. It's also very dangerous, Nathaniel. Because when it happens our brains show us something else. It shows us what we *think* is there, what we *expect* to see, which is why it's so dangerous when we drive, you see? Because we're, say, waiting at a crossing, and we move our eyes to look one way and then the other, but instead of seeing what is there in reality, our brains show us what it expects to see based on what was there before. Sometimes our brains work against us. They blind us to what is in front of us, do you understand?"

Nathaniel shook his head. He had no idea what was going on, but was getting more anxious by the second.

"Nathaniel, I am waiting for a message from someone. I thought it was a text message, but now you're mysteriously here to tell me something. So what I'm seeing is that you are here to give me a message. I know about the plan, Nathaniel, in fact most of it was my idea. It's OK. We can talk about it freely. I'm seeing the reality of what's in front of me, not what I think is there. Are you? Look at what is in front of your eyes. If you're in on it too, and I'm pretty sure that you are, then recognise what you are seeing. If there's something you need to say, then say it. If there's something you need to do, do it."

Nathaniel looked in his face and suddenly felt as if he'd stumbled into an entirely different situation. He didn't believe in a sixth sense – although his belief system had become confused recently to say the least – but in the same way that a person knows they're being stared at in a crowd, or they know who is calling even though they're nowhere near the phone, or they know their twin is ill even though they're on the other side of the world, he knew something. Definitively.

Owens was waiting for a text message about the bombings. A text message from one of the two men. A text message that Nathaniel knew would never come.

This was it. This was the confirmation he'd wanted – *needed* – all along. He was on the right track. Aurora wasn't lying, of course she wasn't lying. He was saving those children.

He was saving Amanda.

Owens was standing so close he couldn't possibly see Nathaniel reach for the gun. He couldn't possibly see the barrel slowly rising and pointing directly at his chest.

And he certainly couldn't possibly see Nathaniel's finger squeeze the trigger.

Nathaniel fired three times in quick succession, just like he had in his office a lifetime ago.

In the milliseconds after the first shot, Owens grabbed hold of Nathaniel, as though embracing him. The way an old man might if he feels a twinge in his chest, fearing the worst. The next two shots caused Owens to squeeze Nathaniel's arm, a look of confusion crossing his face just before he crumpled into a heap at Nathaniel's feet. He still had a strong grip on Nathaniel, who crouched down with him to the ground.

Owens teetered between sitting and lying, between life and death, staring at Nathaniel with a pleading, desperate look on his face. He looked like he was trying to speak, but only a soft, hoarse breath came from his lips.

"Just lie down," Nathaniel heard himself saying, surprised by how dispassionate his own voice sounded. "Not long now, Jonathan. Close your eyes. It won't be long."

The blood seeped into Owens' shirt, the deep red staining the once-white cotton. Nathaniel noticed Owens' red tie was inexplicably the same rich crimson colour as the blood that was seeping out of him.

Owens' body went limp, and his breathing abruptly stopped.

Nathaniel felt the silence envelop him and felt as he had done in the hallway. It was as though the room was suddenly soundproofed. The silence almost hurt his ears.

He wondered how he was even going to begin cleaning the room. And himself.

"You can't clean this up, Nathaniel," Aurora said softly. "If you move him now you'll be covered in blood."

He glanced down at his shirt, amazed that there only seemed to be a minimal amount of blood on him. If he closed his suit jacket, it wouldn't look like anything had happened at all.

"So I just… leave hi— leave *the body* here?"

"Yes. Think about it. If you try and move him you'll be covered in blood. And also, where would you move him? Onto the bed? Into the bath? There's nowhere to hide him, Nathaniel. Nobody knows you're here. The safest thing to do is leave, just like we discussed."

"But…"

He looked at the corpse which, until he had pulled the trigger, was a person. He could still feel the warmth radiating from him.

"Just leave it here?"

"Nathaniel, this was the plan. The only thing you need to do is stand up and leave. Cover your hand with your jacket sleeve when you turn the door handle, and get out of here."

Nathaniel stood, carefully allowing the body to fall fully onto the floor.

She was right. She'd been right all along.

And he had proof now, too – the text message that was being so eagerly anticipated.

That was proof that Nathaniel was on the right path. Not that the text message would ever come through now, given that the only two men in the world who could send it were gone.

He turned towards the door and made the decision. He took a step forward and froze as he heard a notification sound from a mobile phone. Not his.

He swung round to locate the sound, and saw the small black rectangle on the bed light up as a message filled the phone screen.

"Don't," Aurora said, materialising into the room.

"Why is he getting a message? I thought there were only three of them?"

"There were only three of them, Nathaniel. Please leave the phone."

He looked over at Aurora.

"What do you mean, leave the phone? This doesn't make any sense. Why would he still be getting a message? Who else is involved?"

"*Nobody*, Nathaniel. It was just them."

His head swirled with images and thoughts that never seemed to coalesce into anything solid. Ideas and deductions – like pieces of a million different jigsaw puzzles – slid past each other, none of them fitting.

He picked up the phone and read the words on the screen. He couldn't read the whole message as it was only a message preview, but he read enough.

"This isn't about bombing," he said to Aurora accusingly. "This is about a fraudulent business deal."

She nodded.

"I don't understand."

He sat down on the edge of the bed and looked at Aurora.

"Please, Nathaniel," Aurora said. "You have to get out of here now."

He stared through her, trying to piece it together. He'd been looking for evidence this whole time, and was convinced he'd found it. It was how he so easily pulled the trigger this time, in spite of being only inches away from the target of the bullet.

"Nathaniel, it's still all true. There was going to be a bombing campaign and you've stopped it now. You've won. We all have. But you have to get out of here. You have to trust me."

"But... such a protracted campaign... so much planning... so many deaths... How can there be nothing? No indication that it's real?"

His head swam and he felt like he was losing control like he had after he'd hit the fox.

"Nathaniel, you have saved Amanda. You've saved all of them, you need to focus on that. Just because he happened to be waiting for a different text, it doesn't make all of this untrue."

"But how do I *know*, Aurora? How do I know any of it?"

The full impact of the three killings crashed into him like a freight train now. The killings – the murders, because that's exactly what they were – were suddenly real to him. As the relief that Amanda had been saved – if that was even true – washed over him, a new emotion had taken the place of the fear he'd felt.

Guilt.

He had planned the deaths of three people. He'd bought a gun. He'd pulled the trigger and murdered them. And now that it was all over he still had nothing to prove they were going to do what Aurora had said they were going to do. How was that possible? How could there be nothing he could point to as evidence?

Everything was caving in. As if his entire life was built on wooden stalks, and one by one they were rotting away – or being chopped down. The same thought kept playing over in his mind – he'd murdered three people based on what Aurora had said.

Although deep down he knew that wasn't completely true. It wasn't just what she'd said – she'd shown him things, he'd heard the screams. He'd smelled the smoke and felt the intense heat of each and every blast. She'd convinced him then, why was this any different? Why would the fact that the text message wasn't about the bombings feel like such a punch in the gut?

He knew why.

Because he'd been *waiting*. This whole time, he'd been waiting. There'd been a vague hope that at some point he'd find something tangible, some evidence to prove that he was on the right track. And mere minutes ago, he'd got it. The text message that would never come. That would be proof enough. It wouldn't hold up in court, but it'd be enough for him. *He'd* know at least. Getting caught was always a possibility, but as long as he knew that he'd saved Amanda, that was all that mattered.

The absent text message was the evidence he'd needed.

And then it had gone. In an instant, the final wooden stalk holding up the entire house had been shown to be made of cardboard.

So where did that leave him? Was he saving the world, or destroying it?

That's when there was a knock at the door.

Chapter 22

At the sound of reality breaking into the room, Nathaniel froze.

He automatically held his breath, as if breathing would alert whoever was outside to his presence.

He looked over at Aurora. She didn't look concerned, which should have felt reassuring but felt disconcerting.

"Jon!" a voice called from outside.

Aurora put up her hand as if to tell Nathaniel to stay where he was. He was still frozen to the spot, and wondered whether he could even move if he wanted to.

The knock came again, slightly louder this time.

"Jon!" the voice called with a slight urgency.

Nathaniel wondered how this person fit into the puzzle now. Was he part of the fraud? He couldn't have been part of the bombings, as Aurora said they wouldn't happen now. Had he taken too long? Would there be a fourth person now?

The phone in Nathaniel's hand suddenly started vibrating, causing him to jump and almost throw it across the room. He dropped it onto the bed and read the name of the incoming caller. Daryl Simmons. He didn't recognise the name, although that didn't mean they didn't work for the same company. There were so many different offices all over the place that he didn't know a lot of the people.

He let the phone ring out. He looked over at Aurora again, who mouthed the words *It's OK.* He wondered about that.

Was it OK? Could it ever be?

And why had she mouthed the words? Did that mean other people could hear her? Surely he was the only one that could see or hear her?

He didn't know anything anymore. Nothing made sense. He should've felt happy or relieved right now, but instead he felt trapped. Claustrophobic. He wondered how he was going to get out of the room. He looked over at the rapidly cooling body of the man he had just killed. *Murdered.* Even if he did get out of here, there was no way of knowing what would happen next.

Amanda. He just had to focus on Amanda. Whatever happened to him for the rest of his life didn't matter. He'd saved his little girl. Every breath she took now was because he'd saved her. Surely that was the ultimate gift a father could give his child? He was supposed to be the protector, and he'd done that and then some.

The phone screen lit up again, this time with a new message.

It's Daryl. Breakfast? I'll be down there with Kendrick. If not see you at Reg.

Nathaniel allowed himself to breathe. He listened out for some indication that the man – Daryl – had gone. After a few moments he thought he heard footsteps, although couldn't be sure.

Aurora sat next to him.

"He's gone, Nathaniel," she said quietly. "Please. We have to go. We are running out of time."

The swirling emotions in Nathaniel's body didn't allow him to respond. It was as if he was trying to decide which impulse – if any – to follow. It wasn't just the binary choice of fight or flight. He didn't know whether to cry, scream, jump for joy that it was over... Like Buridan's Ass, he sat, paralysed. One question repeated in his mind.

Who even was he at this point?

Aurora spoke again, and when she did, the voice was nothing like Nathaniel had ever heard.

"Nathaniel," she said with a solemnity that Nathaniel didn't recognise. "I can sense how you're feeling. I'm going to show you something now. And then, we have to leave. I've shown you what they were going to do, now I'm going to show you why."

Aurora reached out and touched Nathaniel's forehead, and the world disappeared.

Chapter 23

He found himself in the apartment from last night. No, that wasn't true. He was somehow standing *just outside* but able to see and hear everything through the wall.

The three men he had killed all sat together. Jonathan Owens and Ricky Gardner sat on the sofa, and William Kwang sat opposite them in a chair.

Nathaniel suddenly realised his mental block preventing him from using the men's names was gone. After each killing, he no longer used their names, not even in his own mind, referring instead to each as *the body*. It was as though by not uttering their names he could somehow detach himself. He didn't feel the need to do that now, maybe because they were still alive here. Wherever 'here' was...

The table Nathaniel had seen when he had gone to Gardner's apartment was not there, and he wondered when exactly in time this meeting had happened. Or, if this was another timeline, when in time it would happen.

He paused – the meeting couldn't possibly happen anymore. He had made sure of that. He thought back to the conversation he'd had about quantum systems and how they were never 'real' until somebody witnessed them. Did his act of watching these three men somehow bring them back into reality, or into a reality somewhere? He didn't know, although he trusted that Aurora wouldn't have allowed him to see whatever he was about to see if it would undo all the work they'd done.

He noticed that the television was on, although couldn't make out what was playing. None of the three men seemed to be watching it either.

Nathaniel suddenly realised Owens had been speaking.

"…so it's not about asking for permission to get a message across anymore. It's about delivering the message ourselves. I like the shopping centre idea, but it still doesn't feel personal enough. I don't want it to be seen as an attack on corporations or big business, it has to be *personal*. It's up to us to make real change here."

Gardner nodded.

"This is what I've been saying all along," he said to Owens and Kwang. "They need to understand that nowhere is safe anymore. Whenever people leave the house they're aware of things around them, and half-expecting something to happen. They lock their house, they lock their car, they keep their purses and wallets close to them, they look before they cross the road, they make sure their kids hold their hands, they pause if they smell smoke. People at shopping centres aren't expecting an attack, but they could well be expecting *something*. It needs to be closer to home. And in my opinion, I think that's exactly where we should attack. Their homes."

Owens went to speak.

"I know what you're going to say, Jon, but hear me out. People swan about in their houses as though they've got some kind of a right to safety. As though they were born to be happy and have peace of mind. We want to disrupt things, we want to destroy the order of things, so we need to shake them out of it. What better than to literally hit them where they live?"

"No," Kwang said.

"What do you mean, 'no'?" Gardner spat.

"We've been through this, Rick. That's what I mean. How many more times do we need to tell you that isn't the best way? We shouldn't target houses. Firstly, it would be a logistical and financial nightmare – selecting key people and finding out addresses, getting enough explosives, planting devices according to the particular security systems and protocols they may have when they enter and exit their houses, ad infinitum – and secondly, it'd take too long. There are three of us. Do you have any idea how long it'd take to hurt as many people as we want to? We're talking hours and hours of preparation for just one property, not to menti—"

"Always ready with problems," Gardner scoffed. "Alright then, genius. Do you feel like coming up with any, oh, I don't know, *solutions* this time? Or is it down to me and Jon again?"

Kwang gave a humourless smile.

"I do have an idea actually," he said. "A solution to all of this. Personal, destructive, all of it."

Owens and Gardner waited. Kwang obviously relished the attention, drawing out the silence as if enjoying the anticipation of what he was about to say.

"Which is?" Owens asked impatiently.

Kwang leaned forward and smiled.

"Schools," he said triumphantly.

The other two men looked at each other.

"Schools?" Owens asked.

Kwang nodded again.

"Schools contain many children, yes? And not just children – teachers too. Why target twenty houses with twenty devices when you can target one place – a school – and do the same amount of damage? We want to show society that nothing is safe. So let's hit them where it'll *really* hurt. People think children are innocent. We know they're not, but that's beside the point. What is more unfair or unjust to them all than an innocent being killed?"

A taut silence descended on the three men, and Nathaniel felt the hair on the back of his neck stand up.

Owens looked at Gardner, who in turn looked at Kwang. Nathaniel couldn't tell if they were pleasantly surprised or disgusted by the proposal. Although given all that had happened, he thought he knew which way they would decide.

Kwang continued.

"We want to hurt society, yes? We want to destroy the sense of safety and security that is taken for granted every minute of every day, yes? Then, schools. Anything else is a waste of time."

Owens smiled, Gardner followed suit.

"Alright," Gardner said, "so it looks like you *can* come up with ideas."

"It was that or hospitals," Kwang said coldly. "But hospitals... I don't know, people expect them to die. People prepare for it and, sometimes consciously, sometimes subconsciously, people make their peace with the fact that the person they love might not come out again. We don't want people to be prepared. We want them to feel it in their souls. We want them to be destroyed by it. We want them to never be able to come back from it."

Silence descended onto the room again, and for a moment Nathaniel thought Owens looked scared. An expression formed on his face that Nathaniel recognised from the hotel room. Not quite shock, more disbelief.

Gardner suddenly laughed.

"You are a sick, twisted fuck!" he said, slapping Kwang's shoulder as though they'd been playing football and he'd just scored a goal. "That is perfect. Perfect."

Kwang looked over at Owens.

"Jon? What do you think?"

Owens was staring somewhere into the middle distance. Nathaniel wondered what he was seeing. Was he visualising the attacks? Seeing the mayhem and destruction they were to wreak on the world?

"Jon?" Gardner said. "Are you into this? If not we can go back to the shopping centre idea. I've always liked that one as a—"

"It's remarkable," Owens blurted, as though surprised by his own words. "It is absolutely remarkable. It's everything we wanted, I can't believe we hadn't thought of it before. It's more than destroying safety, it's destroying belief itself. Belief in stability, in order, in God."

"In God? Aren't we getting ahead of oursel—"

"I didn't say destroy God, did I? But belief in Him. There's something existential about the death of a child.

How do you kill someone while keeping their heart beating? You leave them a husk of the person they were and make sure nothing ever fills that husk again. You leave a hole that can't be filled. You take away hope and belief. And what is the most fundamental belief? That someone or something is ultimately in control of all of this. That there is a God, and that He is fair and righteous and just. That He loves you. If we destroy a person's life – burn it to the ground then piss on the ashes – we kill their belief. We kill *everybody's* belief - because if it happened to them, it could happen to you. We make it so horrific that they can't believe God could possibly exist. The result? Carnage. If you destroy hope, belief, order… then you destroy it all."

Owens took a sip of his water. Nathaniel felt physically sick.

"Also," he said casually, "we should film the attacks."

Kwang nodded as though he'd been thinking that all along.

"I agree, Jon. The media will sanitise everything, they will show nothing on the news or their websites. We need our own footage. I have contacts all over the web and the dark web. Distribution will not be a problem. We need the horrors to be inescapable. Whenever the news moves

173

on, we release more footage. Not only do we rip open old wounds, we inflict new ones."

They looked at Gardner, who looked almost euphoric.

"Yes," he said quickly. "To all of it. Yes. This is it, gentlemen. This is how we destroy them."

***

Nathaniel started as if waking from a bad dream, and found himself back in Owens' hotel room, sitting on the bed next to Aurora.

He looked at her.

"Is that… Was that really why they were going to do it?" he asked, knowing the answer.

"Yes, Nathaniel. And you stopped it."

He gave a solemn nod.

"Pure evil," he said, more to himself than Aurora.

"There's more, Nathaniel," Aurora said quietly.

"No, no, please. I don't want to see any more."

"I don't mean that, I mean that their plan went further than they ever anticipated. It might sound dramatic, but the chain of events that the initial bombings put into motion reached into the future more than any of the three men could have imagined. After the bombings, their manifesto was found. Kwang wrote it and spread it on the dark web without the other two knowing. Soon, other bombings begin happening all over the world. Schools first, and then more indiscriminate targets. Shopping centres, sporting events, high streets. There were attacks, fingers were pointed, and then there were counter attacks. Society is held together by the thinnest of threads, Nathaniel. Once a few of them unravel, the whole thing falls apart. It didn't take long to introduce curfews, lockdowns, martial law. It was a perfect storm in the planet's history. A million things came together at once. Death by a thousand cuts, Nathaniel. Those three men wanted people to feel unsafe, and they did it on an unprecedented scale."

Nathaniel saw tears prick Aurora's eyes, and he wondered if she'd not only seen what had happened, but had been there in some way. Maybe she'd lived in some other dimension where this had all happened, where he hadn't stopped it?

"The revenge attacks were brutal. People whose children had died had nowhere to go with their rage, so they became vigilantes, forming mobs. They wanted someone to pay and there weren't enough police or soldiers on the streets to stop them. The anger of grief runs deeper than the ocean, Nathaniel. Put that together with a minimal police presence and a movement of people actively stoking the flames of chaos and equipping others with weapons and you see where it leads. There was a movement and then a counter-movement and nobody knew whose side they were on or what they even believed anymore. We are talking about a domino effect the world had never realised was even possible. The deaths... so many deaths, Nathaniel. It sounds unimaginable, but think about it, every key figure in history started somewhere. We know that just one or two people can change the world. Think about the worst figures in history. Now imagine they can connect online with similar minded people *anywhere in the entire world*, in mere moments."

Aurora paused again, and when she next spoke her voice was much quieter.

"Now imagine they have access to nuclear material."

She looked at Nathaniel.

"Ideas spread quickly, but hate? Hate spreads the fastest. What these three men were to start was not something that could ever be controlled. You didn't just save those children, Nathaniel. You saved everything."

Chapter 24

The realisation of what Aurora was saying was too much for Nathaniel. Once again, he felt as though his body didn't know which emotion to experience first, and so had shut down the capacity to feel any of them.

In an odd way, he felt as though he had become accustomed to knowing when he was in reality, and when Aurora was showing him something outside of it. Everything was as vivid in both places – the things he saw, the things he heard, even his senses of smell and touch – but there was a different *feel* to reality. There was a *density* to it that didn't exist anywhere else. But now... he wasn't sure of anything anymore.

Somewhere from the ether, he felt himself make a decision. He saw himself stand up as if from outside himself. He looked at Aurora.

"Just tell me what to do," he heard his voice say. "I can't think straight. So you tell me what to do next, step by step, and I'll do it."

"Alright, Nathaniel. Pick up a tissue from the bedside table and wipe the mobile phone. Then put the gun in your pocket and tak—"

"Wait," he said. "Not too many things. Slow. Step by step, only. Please."

He took a tissue and wiped the mobile phone, allowing it to drop back down on the bed when he'd finished. What else had she said? Oh yes, the gun. He put it in his pocket. Every movement was slow, as if he was in zero gravity. That's how he felt, as if his mind was on another planet somewhere.

"Well done, Nathaniel," Aurora said kindly. "Now, button your jacket to hide the… the marks on your shirt. We're going to leave now, Nathaniel, so I want you to walk carefully over to the door."

He did as he was told. It felt automatic, not as if he was trying to move his limbs, just that he – somehow – was.

"That's really good, Nathaniel. Now use your sleeve on the door handle to open it. After you do that, step through normally, as if you're leaving your own hotel room. After you step through, allow the door to shut by itself. You don't want to touch the handle with your hand, and you also don't want to risk being seen using your sleeve to move the handle by anyone in the corridor. OK?"

He felt himself nod and did as he was told, following each instruction exactly as Aurora had said. It was nice not having to think, he noticed. It gave him some time to process and calm down.

As soon as he stepped outside the room, he felt as if a spell conjured over him had been broken. A relief washed over him. As the door quietly closed itself behind him, it was as if he was leaving everything in that room. Not just the third and final body, but everything that had happened up to this point. It felt as if he was locking everything away, literally closing the door on a part of his life. He knew it wouldn't be that easy, of course, but that was a thought for another time. Right now, Aurora was in control, and he was doing what she was telling him. He didn't need to focus on the future, he was just living moment to moment, and that was good enough for him.

The corridor felt homely, warm. The soft carpet and décor soothed him in some inexplicable way. It was as if he'd stepped back into the real world, but then it wasn't the real world at all. It was an artist's impression of reality. A sanitised version where everything was soft and inviting.

He felt Aurora's hand on his shoulder.

"Very good, Nathaniel. You're doing really well. Now, all we have to do is walk back to your room. That's all. Does that sound OK?"

He nodded and wasn't quite sure if he actually said "OK" aloud or not, but he definitely thought it.

With every step he took back towards his room he felt calmer and like he was walking back into his life. Putting physical distance between himself and the room was helping. All three men, all their schemes and plans, the visions of the bombings he'd seen, the sounds, the smells, all of it felt like it was in that room. All he had to do now was walk away from it. Get as far away as possible and never look back.

He got to the door of his own room. As he turned the handle it caught on something and he suddenly panicked. The door was locked. Who had locked it and when? After he'd left the room? Did somebody know where he was going? How was that even possible?

"Nathaniel," Aurora said calmly, "you haven't used the key card. Do you know where it is?"

He nodded, and slowly took the card out of his pocket.

"Now slide it in and then turn the handle. You're doing well. We're nearly there."

He did as she said and the door unlocked with a satisfying click. He walked in, pushed the door closed and locked it.

The room looked the same as it had when he'd left, but felt completely different. The bottle of water he'd drank from sat exactly where he'd left it, but he'd been a different person then. That bottle of water was from *before*. There was a *before* version of everything at this point. There was even a *before Aurora*. In each of these periods of time he'd been a slightly different person. He wondered how far he would need to go back before he'd be unrecognisable to who he was now.

He went to sit on the bed.

"Wait!" Aurora said. "You should have a shower, Nathaniel. Undress and put your clothes in the laundry bag which we'll take with us. Remember? Then have a shower and put on the new clothes we brought. Can you do that?"

He nodded. A voice in his head told him that, if he could do the things he'd done over the past two days, then he was definitely capable of having a shower and getting dressed.

He was capable, he thought with a slight shudder, of anything.

Chapter 25

Nathaniel stood in the shower and allowed the hot water to stream down his head, face and body. The water was much hotter than he usually had it, but he didn't bother turning down the dial. After everything he'd done, he wasn't sure he could ever get too clean. In fact, he doubted he could ever be truly clean again. The hotel shower had a little liquid soap dispenser attached to the wall, and he pumped fistfuls of the stuff into his hands, before scrubbing at himself. The bubbles should've felt relaxing and comforting, instead they felt too weak. He wanted something stronger, and an abrasive sponge to scrub himself.

He'd done it. He'd succeeded in his purpose. It just didn't feel like it.

He wasn't sure what he'd expect to feel at this point. It wasn't as if he'd taken control of a plane after the pilot died, or sacrificed himself by jumping on top of a grenade. Nobody knew what he'd done. Although given just *what* he'd done, maybe that was best.

He could cope with what he had done, as long as he knew he'd truly saved Amanda. The way Aurora had explained it was as a form of pre-emptive strike. A defensive move, carried out in advance before any damage was done. There was no way to wait until the bombing campaign happened to take action – that would defeat the whole point. And he couldn't wait for just one of the bombs to go off to prove that he was on the right track. How could he? He couldn't allow a school full of children to die and then stop the men before they got to the next one and the next one. What kind of monster would allow that to happen if they knew they could stop it?

He knew, deep down, that Aurora was right, and had been right all along. He didn't doubt that what she had told him and shown him was true. He knew the bombing campaign would happen if he didn't act, otherwise he'd never have done what he did.

The problem of no evidence bothered him, but not as much as it had done. He had to accept things how they were now. There was no going back. He just had to have faith.

He'd done what Aurora had told him, he just needed to hold on, that it was the right thing to do.

He came out of the shower, towelled off, and began getting dressed. He had brought a navy shirt and black trousers to wear. The concert wasn't going to be a particularly smart occasion, but he always liked to look presentable. If it was a choice between too smart or too casual, he'd choose too smart any day of the week. He felt a tingle of excitement about the concert. It was his return to reality.

He knew how hard Amanda had practised, and knew she'd be great. And not in a father-always-thinks-his-child-is-brilliant kind of way; she did have genuine talent.

He couldn't wait to see his little girl. He'd been to battle for her, his reward would be her beautiful smile and one of her warm hugs. He'd saved his Princess Amanda. He was a good dad.

Maybe in time he would feel proud, he thought. Not right now though. He was essentially still in the battle, still *at the battleground* at least. His next step was to get out of the hotel and get to the concert.

He thought about Vanessa, and was unsure how he felt about seeing her. It would be a relief in a way, and he certainly needed the comforting presence of his wife. Although, is that what it would be? Comforting? Based on their last few interactions, he wasn't so sure.

He wanted more than anything for Vanessa to know what he'd done. To know the lengths he'd gone to in order to save their little girl. To be the protector in spite of the personal cost to him.

And what exactly would that cost be? he wondered. He didn't know enough about forensic science to know what to hide, let alone *how* to hide it. But then Aurora had been guiding him this whole time, so maybe the steps he'd taken at her instruction had been enough? Maybe she was going to take care of the rest?

He didn't know. He just knew that what people think of as control of their own life doesn't exist. How could finite human beings with limited intelligence and unstable emotions ever truly control *anything*? Even with a roadmap of possible outcomes, human beings would still lead with emotion rather than intellect. It's human nature. How else could he explain what he had done? It was *fear*. Fear of losing Amanda, fear of allowing horrific things to happen when he had the power to stop them. Fear of the consequences of his own inaction. Not a calculated move, not a forensic analysis of the situation, but pure emotion. Aurora had been the intelligence, he'd just done what he felt he needed to do.

He thought again about what price he might have to pay. Even if he escaped being caught by the police – which was almost impossible – he would still have to live with himself. He had saved Amanda, yes, and countless other children, and the world - as ridiculous a concept as that seemed to him - but he'd still taken the lives of three human beings. He was a killer now. He'd seen the light go out of the eyes of three people – he'd *made* the light go out. That wasn't something he could shrug off. The end might justify the means, but the means still needs to be reckoned with.

Aurora appeared in the room and smiled.

"Are you feeling better, Nathaniel?" she asked kindly.

He looked at her and realised that with Aurora, it was all or nothing. He had to believe everything or believe nothing. Either he'd genuinely saved the world because of what she'd said, or he hadn't done anything more than kill three people. There was no in-between.

Ultimately, he had to choose what to believe and stick with it.

"Nathaniel," she repeated kindly. "Are you feeling better?"

He thought for a second and nodded. He did feel better. He felt much more himself, and had almost forgotten the wreck he had become in *that* room. It felt like a lifetime ago even though it had been less than an hour.

"That's good," Aurora said. "We should leave now, Nathaniel. The conference starts in an hour so most people will be at breakfast. If we take the back stairs then you can drop your key card in the box at reception."

"Don't I need to tell them I'm going?"

"It's a fast check-out service, you just drop the card in and go. The option is there to speak with someone at the main desk, but…"

He understood.

"But it isn't a good idea for me to be seen any more than necessary?"

"Yes, Nathaniel. The less people who see you here, the better."

He nodded and wondered if this would be his life from now on. Hiding. Avoiding.

Running like a monster from the villagers brandishing pitchforks and torches.

Aurora stood closer to him and put her hand on his shoulder. She looked into his eyes.

"Nathaniel," she said. "Whatever happens from here on out, no matter what, you have to know that this was the right thing to do. I know how this must feel, but you have to hold onto the fact that this was the right thing to do. Please."

"I will," he heard himself say, not quite believing it.

"But you *have* to believe it. Otherwise you'll allow all this, everything that's happened, to consume you. You are not a monster. You did what you had to do to save people you've never met, people you will never meet. Monsters don't do that."

"No, monsters kill people…"

"No, Nathaniel. Don't allow yourself to fall into those thoughts. You have to know that what we did here was the right thing. It's the only way you'll get through. Do you understand? Otherwise you won't make it."

He wasn't sure he did understand. What was she referring to? What did he have to make it through? He decided he didn't want to know. Not now, anyway.

She stared into his eyes and he knew she was reading him.

She gave a warm smile and he felt that uncanny sense of comfort wash over him. He suddenly thought back to the shower and the warm water streaming down his body. That didn't get him clean, but whatever Aurora had just done made him feel cleaner than he had for a long time.

"Let's move, Nathaniel," she said quietly. "I'll tell you what we need to do. There's a lot we have to wipe down and get rid of. We'll do it though, Nathaniel."

He smiled and gave a brief nod.

"Everything *will* be clean again, Nathaniel. Don't worry."

Chapter 26

Vanessa took another sip of coffee – her third cup so far – and sat back into the sofa. Three coffees, and she was still fighting to stay awake. It was going to be a long day.

Since getting up, she'd made breakfast for herself and Amanda, had washed, dried and put away the dishes, cleaned what could only be described as 'detritus' around the living room, and only now had finally sat down. She still wasn't dressed, but that wasn't unusual for this time on a weekend morning. That's what dressing gowns were for anyway.

Amanda had been practising her piano piece on and off since breakfast. She was disciplined enough to get up early to practise, Vanessa noted, but still young and carefree enough to stop to watch TV now and then.

As it should be, she thought. Amanda was a pretty balanced mix of Vanessa's impulsivity and freedom, and Nathaniel's… well, he would call it self-discipline, Vanessa would call it stuffiness. In any case, she seemed to have the balance between work and fun down already. At the age of seven, that was no mean feat.

She checked her emails on her phone to see if anyone important wanted to get in touch. They apparently didn't as all she had were three spam emails and an automated reminder that one of her storecards had an outstanding balance on it.

She checked her news app and scrolled through the various stories. It was nothing good, although when was the news anything other than completely depressing?

She checked it as a habit, not because she wanted to keep particularly informed. She often scrolled through the app, then two minutes later absent-mindedly opened it again. It was something to do more than anything, a way to kill some ti—

A photo next to one of the stories suddenly made her stop scrolling. It showed a fairly nondescript office building with smoke billowing from the windows and huge orange flames licking up the side. The photo had been taken at night, but she recognised the building.

It was Nathaniel's office building.

She felt a sudden surge of panic. She knew Nathaniel was fine, of course, but there was something too close for comfort about it. The building she'd been to numerous times to meet Nathaniel for lunch, or drop him off occasionally, had been engulfed in flames. She knew the layout of certain parts of the building, and had been to the cafeteria countless times. She wondered if any of it was left.

The headline above the photo was characteristically dramatic – *Office block razed to ground in 'mystery fire'*.

She skimmed the article to find out more, but there wasn't much information. The entire building had been 'decimated' after a fire started in the early hours of the morning. It wasn't thought that anybody had been injured as the office was closed. The cause of the fire was being investigated. Scrolling down the feed, another picture showed a blackened husk where the building used to be. Almost comically, the huge sign emblazoned with the company logo still stood in front of it – totally unscathed by the fire, and impotently announcing the company's presence to passing pedestrians and vehicles.

She wanted to call Nathan but thought better of it. Surely he knew, and if he didn't then one of his colleagues or managers would get in touch and tell him about it soon enough. And, on the off-chance that he didn't find out by the afternoon, she'd tell him at the concert.

Something bothered her about wanting to call him, and it dawned on her that she didn't want to call him to let him know about the fire – she wanted to call him to hear his voice and make sure he was alright. It was a pure, almost innocent desire to connect with her husband, a yearning to speak with him that she hadn't thought she'd ever feel about him again.

Even though they were separated, and even though her thoughts and feelings concerning Nathan hadn't been particularly pleasant recently, the thought of a fire tearing through the building in which he worked was... She didn't know exactly. But the various scenarios came thick and fast. What if the fire had happened when he'd been in there? What if whatever had caught fire had done so a few hours earlier? She thought of his organised, buttoned-down temperament and wondered how quickly his composure would evaporate in a life or death situation. It didn't bear thinking about. Nathan wasn't one for dramatic or high-stakes situations.

"Mum?"

She turned to see Amanda staring at her.

"Are you OK? You've gone all still and quiet."

Vanessa smiled, mainly to reassure her daughter but also because she was constantly amazed at how perceptive she was becoming.

"I'm fine," she said, locking her phone and throwing it onto the sofa. "Have you finished practising?"

"Mm-hmm," she said, walking over and plonking herself down on the sofa next to her mum. "Dad told me yesterday that I'll be fine if I just relax. So I'm going to have a break then do a bit more before we go."

Vanessa kissed the top of her head.

"You're going to do so well today. Whatever happens, I'm really proud of you."

Vanessa glanced over at her phone and fought another urge to call Nathan.

"And so is your dad," she added.

She thought back to the photo of Nathan's building, wondering why she couldn't shake the image. She'd already woken up feeling that something was off today, and that Nathan wouldn't make the concert. Finding out about the fire definitely didn't help her state of mind. Although she was exhausted too, which never aided rational thought.

She just hoped Nathan would be at the concert as planned.

And she also hoped that the fire service and police would be able to find out exactly what happened in Nathan's building.

Chapter 27

The first half of the drive from the hotel to the concert was mercifully uneventful. The only reason Nathaniel stopped at all was to get something to eat.

It was only after he'd left his car and started walking into the service station that Nathaniel realised it was coincidentally, the very same service station he'd stopped at on the way to the hotel. Not that he necessarily believed in coincidences – although he wasn't entirely sure what he believed about anything anymore.

He checked himself. Aurora had told him not to think like that. No, he knew what he believed. He'd done the right thing. He needed to see himself as the hero that he was, and not beat himself up.

The cleaner wasn't there, and it showed in the amount of crap all over the floor. Nathaniel chose the same table with the same vantage point as last time. The view was different though, because Nathaniel was. He'd finished his mission.

The soldier victorious from the battle.

The victory felt pyrrhic though, and ever since the hotel room an unformulated question had been gnawing at him. He didn't quite know what the question was, but knew at some point in his life he'd have to acknowledge and answer it.

He thought back to the hotel and the end of his mission. There was no fanfare at the end of it, and the world didn't look in any way 'saved'. Not that he knew what that would even look like. How could it look saved if the events he'd stopped would now never happen? It *shouldn't* look saved, it should look exactly the same. It was like holding an umbrella over an ants' nest. They'll never thank you because they'll never know what the flood would have been like.

The last time he was here he'd thought about Vanessa being in labour, and how everything had changed after Amanda had been born. There'd been a definite before and after, just like there was now.

Although, before and after what, exactly? What was the defining event going to be counted as? Was it him saving the world, or him killing three people? He didn't consider them people, but he wondered whether anyone else would see it that way. One man's terrorist is another man's freedom fighter. Heroism so often depends on which side you're already on.

The future was uncertain to Nathaniel. So was the past, for that matter.

The only thing anyone could ever be sure of was the present, although even then how much could a person trust their own perceptions? Nathaniel had seen theories about life being a simulation, an advanced, seamless system in which nothing was real. And if that were true, how would anyone ever know? If the simulation was good enough, then they wouldn't. Ever.

Dreams aren't dreams when you're in them – they're reality. Or at least, what you perceive reality to be.

He checked himself again.

He couldn't think like this, he knew that some things were real. Nathaniel was certainly real, and so were Vanessa and Amanda. And, even if it turned out life was some kind of simulation, and none of the people in his life actually existed, that would never negate everything. Some things would still be real. His emotions, for instance. How many times had he woken from a dream and still felt the emotions of it reverberating around his body? Even if the cause of those emotions was his subconscious mind as he slept, and even though he knew that what he'd experienced wasn't real, the emotions were still there and very much *real*. The placebo effect works even when you know you're taking a placebo.

His love for Amanda was genuine, true and real. And, after all, isn't that why he had done all this? To save her?

He wondered if he'd go to the same lengths if Amanda was never at risk. He'd like to think he would, although... who knows? He'd stumbled enough times and hesitated enough times, and that had been with the full knowledge that he was saving Amanda. If he knew he was 'only' saving other children, would he have gone through with it?

Again, he'd like to think so, but...

His thoughts drifted to the three men. He wondered where they were now, whether they were anywhere. If there was a hell, is that where they would be? They hadn't actually done anything yet, as far as Nathaniel knew, but they would have done if they'd been allowed to. Did that make them candidates for hell, or was that only for people who had lived long enough to commit their crimes?

And where did that leave Nathaniel? He'd killed three people. Would he be forgiven for what he'd done? Is that how it works, does everything get looked at together? Yes, he'd killed three people, but in doing so he'd saved millions. Surely the ends not only justified the means, but positively obliterated them?

One day he, like everyone, would die. Would there be a reckoning? A weighing up of all he'd done? Religion certainly seemed to think so.

Someone had once said to Nathaniel that they didn't fear death because they'd simply go back to being what they were before they were born. That is, they'd go back to a state of nothingness. That thought terrified Nathaniel. Not existing is all very well if you'd never known consciousness, but after having lived an entire life, how could the thought of an eternity of nothing inspire anything other than terror?

Although, given his current score card, maybe nothingness would be better than the alternative.

He shook his head. He was tying himself up in knots again.

The question that had been simmering under the surface of his consciousness suddenly bubbled up into his conscious mind. It was a simple question – two words only – but with limitless ramifications.

What now?

He'd go to the concert, of course. He'd see his lovely Princess Amanda, and try and patch things up with Vanessa.

That didn't feel like the totality of the answer though. The question wasn't about what he did next, it was about how he would live with himself now. It wasn't so much about what he would do, more about who he was. He'd crossed a line that human beings don't cross without consequences. And he'd done it three times. Whether people believed in a soul, or a connection with an external source of consciousness, or even just that everything comes from the brain, he'd quenched 'it' three times. That wasn't something that got shrugged off.

And yet... What he did couldn't be viewed in a vacuum. He hadn't gone on some killing spree for his own sick pleasure. It was a mission. A task. It was his purpose. He didn't *want* to do it, he wasn't even sure he *could*, but he kept going because he'd seen the destruction that would be wreaked if he didn't. The worse crime would have been inaction. The worse punishment than having to live with the consequences of his mission would be living with the consequences of *not* going through with his mission. Who could stand and watch the world burn to the ground, knowing they could have stopped the initial spark?

"Nathaniel?"

The voice came from behind him. Like some kind of supercomputer with voice recognition software, his brain ran through the accent, tone and pitch of the voice. The voice was male, with an accent he'd place somewhere in northern England. But other than that, he had no idea who it could be. It definitely wasn't Gary again.

"Nathaniel Bennett?"

The second mention of his name didn't give any more information as to the identity of the speaker, but it did tell Nathaniel something. The person who had spoken was friendly. He wasn't about to be arrested. Nathaniel had never been questioned by the police before, but he imagined their tone of voice would be less friendly and more assertive.

Nathaniel slowly turned and saw an older man wearing a crumpled suit, walking over to him. He had his hand outstretched. For a second, Nathaniel worried he was being targeted by another salesman-cum-zealot.

"I thought that was you," the man said happily. Nathaniel stood and the man read something into his facial expression.

"You don't remember me, do you? We met at the last one of these boring things. I gave a speech about the future of the company and you gave me quite a grilling in the Q and A session later, if I remember correctly."

Nathaniel tried to gather his thoughts. How would he explain being here without mentioning the conference? Although technically they were miles away and on a motorway service station, so Nathaniel could've been heading anywhere.

"I'm not going to the conference," he suddenly blurted.

"Oh? Just thought you'd drive up to the old services and partake of some of their finest nutrition, then?"

Nathaniel froze. The man laughed heartily.

"Just joshing, Nate. What brings you here?"

At that, Nathaniel remembered him. He was the only delegate at the conference – in fact the only person *anywhere* – who decided he was close enough to Nathaniel to use a shortened version of his name without asking. And he *had* grilled him at the last conference, mainly because his speech had been a load of optimistic rubbish about a company whose CEO and board of directors made nonsensical decisions from their ivory towers – probably somewhere in the Cayman Islands – without knowing the first thing about the actual day- to- day running of things.

"I'm just… my daughter has a school concert—"

"All the way up here?"

"What? No, back in London. But I… had to pick up some things to take there."

"You didn't have to pick up the piano, did you?"

Nathaniel chuckled awkwardly, mainly in the hope that it might shorten this exchange.

"No, I didn't have to pick up the piano. We've got some relatives up here, and my little girl left her favourite dress so I've come to pick it up and take it back for her."

"Pretty last minute, isn't it?"

Nathaniel shrugged.

"Daughters," he said. "What can you do?"

"Well, I don't know about daughters but my three sons certainly keep me on my toes, so I sympathise, Nate."

"Well, it was nice seeing you. I better get back."

"Of course. Don't want to miss the concert and get into trouble! I understand. It's a shame you're missing the conference though. You'll miss all the rampant speculation about the fire."

"Fire?"

Nathaniel's mind flashed back to the hotel room and the comment his last target – last *body* – had made about a fire somewhere.

"Yes, at one of the offices. I heard about it from Sean this morning, he said he saw it on the news."

"Which office was it?" Nathaniel asked carefully, not fully knowing if he wanted to know the answer or not.

"Clapham, I think."

"Clapham? That's my office."

"I thought you were North London?"

"No, I'm... no, south. Clapham. When did this happen?"

"I'm sorry, Nate. I had no idea that was your office. Haven't they got in touch with you?"

"My phone hasn't been on much. I didn't want it to distract me from the drive up here."

"Of course, the dress. Well, the fire happened this morning. Very early from what I understand, which is a blessing because it means there'd be no bodies inside."

Nathaniel stared at him.

"What did you say?"

The man stepped back, obviously startled at something in Nathaniel's face.

"I said it was a blessing."

"No, after that."

"Erm…" the man paused. He looked like a child trying to recite his multiplication table in front of the class. "I said, that, it was a blessing because there'd be nobody inside. Because it was early."

"Nobody?"

"What do you mea— yes, Nate, there'd be nobody inside because it was so early in the morning. None of us have to work through the night in any of the offices, so that's a blessing. That's all I was saying. Sorry, did I offend you?"

"No, you didn't," Nathaniel said, wanting to use the man's name but realising he'd never asked and couldn't remember. "It's fine, um, mate."

"Are you alright, Nate? I'm sorry, this must be quite a shock. Maybe you should call head office. Although I'm sure they'll be in touch soon if they haven't tried already. Nobody knows how the fire started so there's likely to be a lot of questions from the fire service. And the police, obviously."

"The police?" Nathaniel blurted before he could stop himself.

"Well, yes, they'll need to investigate in case it was an insurance thing, you know, burn the whole place down and collect the insurance. All that jazz."

Nathaniel nodded slowly. He felt unmoored again. It was a disconcerting sense that he had somehow detached from his surroundings. Like a tugboat in the midst of a raging tempest. Blown about randomly.

No, Aurora has told him not to do this. His mind turned to getting to Amanda.

Feeling a sudden urgency, he started putting on his jacket.

"Thanks for letting me know," he said, hurriedly. "I'll give head office a call and see what they say."

"Yes, I would. As I say, I'm sorry for being the one to break the news to you, Nate. Terrible thing, fire. Makes you wonder what they built the office out of, if it could be destroyed so quickly."

"Mmm," Nathaniel said. "Wait. Destroyed?"

"Yes, as I understand it there isn't much left to even investigate. The police's job should be pretty quick because there won't be much to sift through. Or would that make it slow..? Either way!"

Nathaniel continued getting his things together.

He held out a hand for the man to shake.

"Nice to see you, mate. Thanks for telling me about the fire, and I might see you at the next conference."

"Hope so, Nate. We can catch up next time."

"Sure," Nathaniel said, as he rushed to the exit.

Chapter 28

Nathaniel put his foot down and felt the car roar along the road as he picked up speed.

Not that there was anything wrong with driving fast, but within the speed limits. The difference was he was being erratic and he knew it. He couldn't shake the sense that he was being followed. Not literally, he didn't think that there was a police car behind him, but he had a definite sense of being pursued. That was the only way he could describe it.

He saw himself as an animal just out of reach of its prey. And that whatever was holding the predator back wouldn't last forever, so he needed to make the most of the time he had before he went from potential to actual prey.

His focus this far had been the three men, now it was all about Amanda. He didn't know if the police or whoever might catch up with him, but in a sense he didn't care anymore. His little girl was safe now. All he wanted was to spend as much time with her as he could before… well, before he couldn't anymore.

The rest of the journey flew by and before he knew it, Nathaniel was taking the final exit to get off the main road.

As he slowed the car and turned the wheel, Aurora appeared.

"You're doing well, Nathaniel," she said in her ethereal, soothing voice. "You've come so far since we first met."

He glanced over at her in the passenger seat. Something about her tone was different. He'd been waiting for her to materialise so he could ask her about the fire, but got the sense there was something more pressing to discuss than that.

"Thank you," he said quietly. "So… what happens now?"

"Now you get to go to the concert and see Amanda. You did it, Nathaniel. You saved her, you saved them all."

He couldn't shake the feeling that something wasn't quite right.

"What's wrong, Aurora?"

"Nothing is wrong, Nathaniel. Everything is happening perfectly. What needed to be fixed has been fixed. Because of you. I'm so proud of you, Nathaniel. I'm aware that you sense I'm going to say something that you don't want to hear. And you're right."

He drove in silence for a few moments, processing what she had said and wondering whether to ask the obvious question.

He did.

"What do I not want to hear, Aurora?"

"You know, Nathaniel."

He glanced over at her. He suddenly did now.

"You're leaving?" he asked, almost in a whisper.

"For a time, Nathaniel."

"How long?"

"You'll be fine, Nathaniel. Not seeing me is not the same as me not being here. Does that make sense?"

He nodded.

"Nathaniel, I'm going to do something now. Alright?"

"Yes."

With that, time stopped.

Every car on the road, including Nathaniel's, was immediately stationary. There was no movement, no sound, nothing. It was as if they had dropped into a painting. Life was no longer fluid, it was a tableau.

Nathaniel realised that he could move, but the steering wheel was locked in position.

He turned to Aurora.

"Nathaniel. You did it. Do you understand? No matter what happens, you have saved so many innocent lives. No matter what, take this for what it is."

"What is it?"

She touched his forehead and he sensed a word being spoken into his mind. As if a million voices whispered the word all at once.

Victory.

Aurora smiled.

"That's what it is, Nathaniel. Victory. Remember it, come what may."

"I will."

He paused.

"What do you want to ask me, Nathaniel?"

"You keep saying 'no matter what'. Why do you keep saying that? What are you preparing me for?"

She smiled.

"I can't tell you what will happen, Nathaniel. And in some ways, I don't quite now. I have a mission just like you. I also need to take a number of things on faith. I don't know everything, I only ever know enough. Same as you."

For some reason her words comforted him, even though she'd basically told him that she had no idea what was in store for him.

"OK," he said quietly. "OK. Thank you for being honest with me."

"I'm always honest with you, Nathaniel."

He nodded, and felt a slight twinge of guilt for all the times he'd doubted her.

"Nathaniel, I need you to put your hands back on the steering wheel. I'm going to count down from three to one, and when I get to one everything will start again. You need to be ready because it means the car will start moving at speed just like it was."

"OK," he said, putting both hands on the steering wheel and trying to remember how much pressure he had been putting on the pedals at his feet.

"OK, Nathaniel. Three… Two… One."

In an instant the world begun again, and Nathaniel heard the roar of the engine as his foot pressed too hard on the pedal. At the same time, he fought to straighten the car and swerved slightly. He eased off the pedal and righted the car.

He didn't look towards the passenger seat.

He didn't need to.

He couldn't feel Aurora anymore. She was gone.

Chapter 29

After dropping off Amanda, Vanessa hurried round to the hall to find her seat. As she walked down the corridor to the back, she secretly hoped she'd get there and find Nathan was already seated. He already had his ticket, so unless he'd lost it – and Nathan never lost *anything* – it was possible he'd got in and taken his seat already.

She still couldn't quite pinpoint why the fire had shaken her. Most of the time she felt as though she didn't even like Nathan anymore, why would a fire at his office – in the early hours of the morning when nobody could possibly have been there, no less – affect her so much? Hearing the vague sounds of children rehearsing, instruments clanging and piano keys being hit, and watching the parents kissing their children goodbye and wishing them luck, she thought she might know.

Amanda.

It wasn't that she was worried she would lose Nathan, it was that she was worried that Amanda would. She knew how much Amanda loved her dad, and how much he loved her. The fear wasn't the fire— she knew the odds of

Nathan suddenly dying in a fire or being swept away by a tsunami were miniscule. But there was one way Amanda could lose her dad, one very easy way. Divorce. And Vanessa was the one who could make it happen. The threat wasn't that Amanda would lose her dad in an office fire. The threat was Vanessa, and what she might decide.

She stepped into the hall and weaved through the sea of other parents to find her seat, smiling and waving half-hearted hellos to some of them on the way. As she got closer to her row of chairs she could see that Nathan hadn't arrived yet, or at least if he had, he hadn't taken his seat.

If he was late, or didn't arrive, Amanda would be crushed, which meant that Vanessa would be too.

But that was another thing that didn't make any sense – she knew Nathan was dependable, why did she keep having thoughts that he wouldn't turn up today? Nathan was many things, but a deadbeat dad wasn't one of them. Maybe the separation was getting to her more than she cared to admit, especially now that her working life had turned to crap as well.

Maybe she *wanted* Nathan to be a bad dad?

Was that it? Did she want him to play to the stereotype of the loser dad so that divorcing him would be easier? It was certainly easier to accept than depriving

Amanda of her dad because Vanessa didn't find him exciting or adventurous enough.

But then, what was justification for a divorce? She didn't want to have to wait for years to pass until Amanda left home, or until Nathan did somehow turn into a bad dad. She'd already felt the best years of her life had slipped away, she didn't want to waste any more of them.

She wondered how much was she willing to sacrifice for her daughter, and whether she could put up with a mediocre husband if it meant her daughter would have a great dad.

But that wasn't fair. What about Vanessa's life? What about her dreams and goals?

She knew what her mum would say about that.

You should've thought of that before you married him.

Vanessa knew that nobody ever thinks like that. People might have a fleeting thought about what their partner will be like as a parent, but in the giddy first throes of a new romance and in the circus that is getting engaged and planning a wedding and a honeymoon, nobody stops to think about the boring things. Who stops to think about the mortgage, or which parent is going to be the better one, or whether getting a pet will be a good idea? Only the most calculating people would do that, everybody else is too busy enjoying the ride. At least they should be. Vanessa certainly had been.

At the start of the relationship she couldn't believe how lucky she was to find somebody like Nathan right at the time she needed him most. If they had met a few years earlier or a few years later, the moment either wouldn't have arrived yet or would have passed. She'd often compared it to two trapeze artists swinging by their feet and trying to grab each other's hands. They had to meet at just the right time, just the right angle, in just the right conditions. If they tried to grab too early, they'd miss. Too late, they'd miss too. She wondered how many people had missed *the one* by virtue of bad timing.

She wondered if she had.

She took her seat and hoped she didn't look too conspicuous there without Nathan. She didn't want people to jump to conclusions and have hushed conversations about them. She looked around and smiled at a few familiar faces – nobody whose names she knew, just parents she'd seen here and there. She kept glancing over at the doors, hoping Nathan would walk through.

For Amanda's sake, she kept telling herself. Just for Amanda.

"Excuse me," a voice said.

She turned and saw an older man. He looked more like a grandfather than the father of one of the school children. In fact, looking more closely, she wondered if he was a great- grandfather.

"Hello," she said.

"Sorry to bother you, but is anybody sitting in this seat?"

He indicated to the seat next to her. Nathan's seat.

"Oh, sorry, that seat's taken."

"My apologies. Your husband?"

Vanessa paused. What exactly was Nathan? Technically they were still married, but they were separated. He wasn't her ex, and even if he was she suddenly realised how uncomfortable she would be to call Nathan her ex-husband.

She smiled and gave the man a small nod.

He smiled back and walked away. Vanessa didn't have the heart to tell him that if he hadn't bought a ticket he probably wouldn't find a seat anywhere, unless someone didn't show up. Although, she thought, what sort of person wouldn't buy a ticket? And what sort of person wouldn't turn up to see their own child perform in a concert, rendering the ticket spare?

She gave a nervous glance at the door. On not seeing Nathan, she felt another emotion.

Excitement.

In spite of wanting Nathan to be there for Amanda, in spite of worrying about him and the fire, in spite of it all, a part of her – a *huge* part of her now that she was admitting it – wanted Nathan to not turn up. She wanted a concrete, solid reason to point to and say 'that's it, that's why I'm justified in divorcing this person'. She had her reasons and her complaints, but she couldn't fault him as a father. She wanted that last domino to fall so she could hang an entire divorce on it.

In truth she wasn't sure whether she wanted to divorce Nathan or not – at least if he did something big like letting Amanda down, or having an affair, she'd have her answer. As it was, divorcing her husband and going through custody and whatever-else-divorce-involves battles didn't seem justified.

Razing her life to the ground would be one thing, but doing it and realising it was a huge mistake would be quite another.

It was like her workplace. Yes, it was crap at the moment, but not bad enough to justify actually leaving and having the stress of trying to find something else. Updating her resume, applying for other jobs, going to interviews and pretending to be someone she wasn't. It was tiring just thinking about it. And realistically, how many interviews did she think she was going to get at this point in her life..? Modesty aside, she knew she'd let herself go, and as a single mother going through a divorce, how much of a 'catch' would she appear to be really?

She noticed the old man had found a seat next to someone. If he could find a partner, she thought drily, then maybe so could she.

She took out her mobile phone and tapped on her news app to see what else had been said about the fire. Her stomach dropped as she read the latest development.

Body found in remains of office blaze.

Reading the details of the story raised more questions than it answered. The body had been found in an office cupboard, and according to the police the cause of death wasn't the fire or anything related to the fire such as smoke inhalation. They weren't disclosing the details, but the article mentioned 'suspicious circumstances' at least three times.

Vanessa read on, wondering whether this story was related to her sense that Nathan wouldn't be coming today. He was safe, she knew that, but somewhere in her mind she felt there must be some link between the fire and her feeling that Nathan – who was never late for anything – might not arrive for the concert.

She read the article again, then again, hoping to find an answer to the question screaming through her mind.

What *exactly* was going on?

Chapter 30

Nathaniel pulled into the school's car park and managed to grab one of the last parking spaces. He turned off the engine and sat for a moment.

Aurora's absence felt perversely like another presence in the car. He wasn't sure of the mechanics of that – how someone not being there could carry the same weight as someone being there – he just knew that was how it felt.

It reminded him of those times he'd wake up in the middle of the night and forget he wasn't lying next to Vanessa for a brief moment. He'd reach out an arm and find a cold sheet, or the empty space as his arm arced down the side of the bed. And the absence of his wife there would feel as tangible as if she had been there. The emotion was different of course – negative rather than positive – but the weight of it, the *meaning* of it, was as strong as if his arm arced and found the small of her back, the warmth of her shoulder.

Thinking about Vanessa made him painfully aware that he hadn't seen her or Amanda since he'd started – and finished – his mission. He had wondered whether he'd feel a sense of achievement or triumph, the knight in shining armour having vanquished the foes and returning to his now-safe kingdom. He wasn't sure, and wondered again if it was more likely to be a pyrrhic victory.

He did feel satisfied though. Sitting in his car and looking around at the empty vehicles parked all around, he knew that each one, on entering the car park, would have contained one or two proud parents, the child who would be performing, and untold brothers and sisters. It was impossible to know just how many lives he'd saved, and in how many different ways he'd saved them. Not just the children themselves, but the parents, the siblings, the friends of the family, the wider communities.

And, if what Aurora had said was true – and he didn't doubt it was – he'd saved more than that.

He got out of his car and walked into the school, absorbing the sights and sounds of this world he had saved. The notices on the boards in the corridor, the various sports trophies that the school teams had won, the drawings and paintings displayed outside classrooms giving a snapshot of the beautiful little souls that inhabited each one. It suddenly dawned on him, that this was very much part of his victory party.

Of course, the real reward would come later when he saw his Princess Amanda, safe and happy and playing the music that she so loved. Safe from those three men, forever.

He found the main hall and stood at the back, scanning the rows for his seat. He saw the back of Vanessa's head and felt a jolt of nerves tinged with excitement.

He was a different man now. He'd saved their daughter and proved himself. He was a hero.

He just wouldn't ever be able to tell either of them.

As he made his way to the row of seats, he kept glancing at Vanessa, as if willing her to turn around. Her head was tilted down slightly. She either had something on her mind or was looking at something on her lap.

He wondered how she would respond when she saw him. She'd probably give one of her clipped smiles, as if she wanted to be genuinely happy but couldn't quite allow herself to be. Maybe that's how she felt about him now – that she didn't love him anymore but wanted to. At least he hoped that's how she felt, the alternative was that she didn't love him anymore and no longer cared, which would obviously have been worse.

He got to the end of the row and began walking towards Vanessa. She looked up as though sensing him there, stood up and embraced him. She squeezed hard and Nathaniel smelled the heady, intoxicating scent of her shampoo mixed with her perfume. It was the same scent he'd imagined back in the hotel in London after leaving the first *body* in his office cupboard. It felt like a lifetime ago.

Three lifetimes ago, to be exact.

"Hi," Nathaniel said. "This is… nice."

She suddenly broke away. Her facial expression was one of surprise. She looked to Nathaniel as though she'd woken up the day after a party having realised what she'd done the night before.

"Sorry," she said, smoothing her top as though it would have somehow got crumpled. "I… don't know why I did that."

"We *are* married," Nathaniel said, "I'm sure nobody minds."

A look flashed across her face that Nathaniel couldn't quite read. He wondered if it was embarrassment, although if it was the source of it wasn't clear to him. They were still married, after all.

"It's good to see you, Vanessa."

"You too, Nathan."

They held eye contact for a while. Nathaniel desperately wanted to tell her everything that had happened, not just because he wanted her to know how far he'd gone to save Amanda, but because their embrace was the first time he'd received the welcome touch of another human being for what felt like a decade. He suddenly realised what he wanted – needed – was physical intimacy with another human being. He thought back to the last person he'd touched, and who had touched him. There had certainly been no comfort for him in that encounter.

He needed a hug, or a pat on the shoulder. He'd probably have settled for a mere handshake a few moments ago. But the feel of Vanessa's embrace had reminded him of the inexorable power of physical closeness with another person. He felt like a starving man who'd got accustomed to his hunger, then was given a tiny morsel to eat. Rather than sating his appetite, or diminishing it, it simply served to ratchet it back up to unbearable levels.

"Shall we sit?" Vanessa asked, breaking into his thoughts. He noticed she had sat down while asking the question, which had obviously been purely rhetorical.

Nathaniel nodded and followed her lead. He didn't want to mention that she had already been sitting down as she still seemed embarrassed.

Once again the impulse to tell her everything flooded over him. He'd always felt a curious sensation when they argued at a distance. While not together, he'd fume and seethe, and imagined that she would do the same. But the moment they were physically together in the same place again, the positives would outweigh the negatives. Being in the presence of the woman he loved somehow quelled the anger in an instant. He'd been angry with Vanessa, and had wondered about divorce and the million ways she would try to hurt him or stop him seeing Amanda. But now that they were together, physically, in the same space, all of that faded away. Maybe there was some unknown chemical connection between partners, or maybe the theoretical is always less potent than the actual.

He just wanted to weep in Vanessa's arms while at the same time tell her about how he had vanquished the foes at their gate. How he had selflessly stood up and destroyed the threat to their lives, to their daughter.

He wanted to both confess and boast.

"So," Vanessa said awkwardly, "are you ready for the recital?"

"Yes, I think so. It's a concert though."

"What do you mean?"

"It's technically not a recital, it's a concert."

Vanessa gave a grin.

"What on earth is the difference?"

"A recital is just one or two performers, but there are fourteen kids doing different compositions today, so it's definitely a concert."

Vanessa gave an odd look.

"Are you serious?" she said with a wry smile. "How do you even know that?"

He shrugged.

"I read up on it when Amanda told me about it. Then I did a load of research so I could calm her down if she started getting nervous and worrying she was going to mess up. The more performers, the less is on one person's shoulders. So the less there is to be nervous about. The recital or concert thing was just something I picked up on the way. I suppose. I don't really remember."

Vanessa smiled, and so did Nathaniel. He was experiencing one of those rare 'husband' moments where he'd apparently done the right thing but had no idea what it actually was.

They sat for a while as the hall filled up and members of a brass band filtered onto the side of the stage. They were obviously kids from the school, but all looked slightly older than Amanda. As each one took their place, they fiddled with their instruments and studied their sheet music as though about to play Carnegie Hall. Nathaniel liked that. They were school kids but had a level of dedication and professionalism that he admired. It was something he had tried to instil in Amanda, and based on her excellent grades and the fact she was playing in the concert, he thought he was doing a pretty good job of it.

The heavy doors of the hall clanged shut behind them, and the pre-show murmuring began. It always sounded the same to Nathaniel, he could be watching a West End musical, a small amateur dramatics production, or sitting in the audience at a work conference. No matter where he was, the pre-show murmuring always sounded the same.

He noticed Vanessa fidgeting and every so often glancing over at him. He got the feeling that he wasn't the only one who wanted to get something off his chest today, although he supposed that anything Vanessa had to say wouldn't necessarily be what he wanted to hear.

"Nathan," she whispered, suddenly turning around. "I know things have been… how they've been. But are you OK?"

He thought for a moment, and realised he had no idea how to answer that question.

"I mean," she continued, " I heard about your office and everything. That must have been a real shock."

He nodded.

"Yes," he said quietly, "it was."

"Are you OK?" she repeated, even gentler this time. "It's just so tragic."

"No, it's.. it's fine. It's bricks and mortar. I'll work from home or from one of the regional offices. It might take some time to rebuild everything but they will, and I'll be back in like nothing ever happened.   I wouldn't say it's tragic. They're certainly insured…!"

She gave him a look as though he was answering a different question.

"Nathan," she said gently, "don't you know?"

"Know what?" he asked, dreading the next words that might come out of her mouth.

The band started playing a loud, bombastic tune as the lights in the hall dimmed and the headteacher took to the stage.

"Ladies and gentlemen, welcome to the show!"

The band roared into an even louder number, and multicoloured lights swept across the stage and the audience.

"Know what?" Nathaniel repeated, in an odd whisper-shout. He heard the urgency in his own voice then, making him even more anxious like some sinister feedback loop of fear.

Vanessa leaned over, flooding his senses once again with her perfume-and-shampoo scent. It was calming, familiar.

He had no idea it was merely lulling him into a false sense of security.

"Nathan," she whispered into his ear, "they found a body. Somebody died."

Nathaniel felt the blood drain from his face.

"And it doesn't look like the person died in the fire, either. They seem to think he was killed before. They... they think it's murder. Someone was killed, Nathan. Deliberately."

An icicle playfully sliced its way down Nathaniel's spine, following the contours of his back as though enjoying the route. It somehow managed to both freeze and burn his flesh all at the same time.

The band kept playing, the music drowning out the incomprehensible sound that Nathaniel felt come out of his mouth.

Chapter 31

For an awful moment, Nathaniel thought he'd be sick.

In the same way that a child might cry for their mummy, he suddenly pined for Aurora. She would explain what was going on, or at least calm him down. Why would this be the point she'd disappear on him? When he needed her most?

He waited a moment, as though the severity of the situation might somehow persuade her to come back from... wherever she was. He closed his eyes, willing her to show up, to put a hand on his shoulder and ease the myriad emotions and thoughts that swirled and ricocheted around his soul.

But Aurora wasn't around. She'd gone.

Nathaniel sat, stunned, and watched the members of the band as if through smoked glass. He felt like he had back at the hotel, although this time Aurora wasn't there to bring him back.

He had the strange sensation of knowing he could hear the music, but not registering it. His ears worked and so did his brain, but he couldn't detect tone or pitch or rhythm. It was nothing but static.

A radio tuner stuck between stations.

Empty. Formless.

Meaningless.

"Nathan, are you alright?"

In the same way as he knew he could hear the music, he knew that he had heard Vanessa's voice, but there was no meaning behind it. Just sounds.

"Nathan," she said with panic in her voice, "are you alright?"

He felt her hand on his arm, and smelled her familiar scent again as she leaned towards him. For the briefest moment he was jolted back into reality.

"I'm… shocked," he said, somehow managing to string two words together.

"Of course you are. It must be a big shock. Do you think you knew the person?"

He felt an intention to shake his head, but wasn't sure if he actually followed through with it in the real world.

"Nathan, did you know him? Was he one of your employees?"

The panic rose up in him now, coming out as anger.

"Why would I know him? Why would I have anything to do with this? How would I know, Vanessa?"

He watched as his wife physically recoiled, and immediately regretted the ferocity of his response. Like an old drunk somehow momentarily shocked into sobriety, he totally came back to himself.

"Sorry," he said quickly. "It's not your fault. It's…"

The old Vanessa returned then. Not the compassionate one, but the aggressive one. The one who had kicked him out, the one who was pushing for a divorce.

"I was just asking," she spat at him, "surely hardly anyone would be there that time of the morning. You're supposed to be one of the managers, why *wouldn't* you know who was working then? Do you know how worried I've been about you, Nathan? I've been worried sick."

"Vanessa…"

She folded her arms, and just like that, the fight started and finished.

***

Nathaniel watched the rest of the concert in a daze, checking his watch and hoping Amanda would be on soon. He wasn't sure how much time he had left.

He wondered about the body – *the body* – he'd locked in the cupboard. Would that mean it'd be protected from the fire, or exposed to even more heat than if he'd, say, just left it on the floor? It didn't seem like a fireproof

231

cupboard, just a standard one.   Given that Nathaniel worked for an office supply company, he should've known, but the level of fire safety of any given product wasn't exactly his area of expertise.

He sat tight, every so often checking the time as if it wasn't an empty and futile gesture.

Glancing over at Vanessa, he fought an almost overwhelming compulsion to tell her everything.   If she understood all he'd done and been through there's no way she'd be angry with him.   She might even back him up and provide an alibi.

A new sense of fear pulsed through him.

Was that what it was going to come to? Needing an *alibi*? Giving a statement and accounting for his actions over the past forty-eight hours?   Fingerprints and mugshots? Interrogations and legal representation?

Of course he knew he might get caught and need to speak with the police.   He knew all of that.   The difference was, up until this point he knew that if any of that happened he'd have Aurora by his side.

She was a buffer.   A wall between himself and the actions he'd taken.

He realised he'd been functioning in a state of denial.   He'd looked away from his own actions in an attempt to make them not exist.

And if nobody observes something, then it doesn't exist. That's what Gary said. Well, what if only *two* people witnessed it, and one looked away and the other was now dead? Did it still happen? Did it still exist?

His panicked brain merged his thoughts once again into philosophical nonsense, although one fundamental truth certainly remained.

Aurora was gone. He was on his own.

Or was he? He looked back at Vanessa.

Maybe he should tell her and at least that way he'd have someone in his corner. And he'd be a hero in her eyes then, not an annoyance or a disappointment or whatever else she thought of him at times like this. A hero who had saved their daughter. Who had saved millions.

He watched as she huffed and puffed, and gave him periodic dirty looks. The smartest move would be to not rush into anything, to keep his mouth shut. He couldn't remember the last time he'd kept a secret from her. And he'd never kept one as life-changing as this.

It created a strange dynamic. He knew something she didn't, something that once she knew she could never un-know. It was almost something that gave him a certain amount of power – not that he felt particularly powerful at this moment in time. He could change her life – all their lives – in an instant by merely telling her something he knew that she didn't.

Holding back was almost physically painful. From a distance – via text message or even by phone – keeping a secret was easy. There was no pressure to play a role, or at least if there was, it was limited. But sitting next to someone, the person closest to you in the world, and not telling them something fundamental about yourself was a battle for which he was woefully unprepared. He didn't know how people could have affairs or lead double lives for years on end – it'd eat him alive.

He looked over at Vanessa. She would understand, he suddenly thought. He had no choice anyway, he was cornered. It was just a matter of time. He would tell her.

He would tell her everything.

Chapter 32

"Vanessa," he said quietly.

She didn't respond and continued staring absent-mindedly at the stage. She looked rapt, so he thought it was more likely she hadn't heard him rather than that she was ignoring him.

"Vanessa," he said slightly louder, "I need to—"

Suddenly her face broke into a smile and she gave a "Whoop!"

He looked onstage to see Amanda – his beautiful, precious, Princess Amanda – walking onto the stage, and everything else paled into insignificance. He didn't quite know how, but his soul felt better whenever she was around. Even more so than with Aurora.

She gave a quick look at the audience and gave a small wave to someone. It wasn't to Nathaniel or Vanessa, so he assumed it was to one of her friends. That in itself made him proud; it was true what he always said to her, everybody loved Princess Amanda. He heard his own words echoed back to himself in his mind – "Why does everybody love Princess Amanda? Because Princess Amanda is lovely."

And she was, he thought, she absolutely was.

She reached the piano and took her seat on the stool. She was at an odd angle, so not quite facing the audience but at the same time not completely side-on either. Nathaniel had a good view, in fact, she was almost angled perfectly towards her parents.

She looked nervous, Nathaniel noticed. Vanessa must have noticed too, because she waved to Amanda and, once she had her attention, gave an excited double thumbs up.

So did Nathaniel. He saw her face light up when she saw her daddy there to support her. He knew in that instance it was worth it. No matter the consequences.

A hush fell over the hall, and Amanda began playing. In an instant, Nathaniel was taken back to all the times he had sat with her as she'd dropped a note here, or hit the wrong note there. There was a bittersweet nostalgia to it. Those times had come before the separation. Before Aurora too.

Before Amanda's daddy had crossed a line and become a killer. Then crossed it again. Then again. Even though he didn't regret what he had done, he missed the time before all of this had happened, and felt a yearning to go back to what – at least in his mind – was a simpler time. He knew it hadn't been really, that the problems with

Vanessa leading to the separation had been brewing for years, and that in some way, it must have been predestined that Aurora would turn up too. He didn't understand how it all worked, but surely even before Nathaniel knew about his mission, Aurora knew that he would accept it, and succeed.

Or maybe not. Maybe his success or failure was up in the air until he'd achieved it. He didn't know, but now wasn't the time or place to be falling back into pondering the space-time continuum, or any of that scientific or philosophical stuff.

He watched Amanda as she played, studying her as she gracefully hit the right notes and every so often smiled. He knew she couldn't wait to tell him later about how nervous she had been but how great it had all gone.

He felt a deep nostalgia, but surprisingly realised it was for the present. He knew he would look back at this time and miss it. Sitting here, watching Amanda, knowing he had saved her, sitting with his wife who may or may not be his wife for much longer. He'd miss it, all of it. Not for the first time, he wondered whether this was the point in his life he'd look back on as being the part before everything collapsed in on him.

Everyone had that moment in their life, they just never knew about it. One day will be the best that life will ever be, and the person whose life it is won't know.

Similarly, one day will be the worst day, he thought, and things would only be better from there. Nobody knows, which is one of the greatest and most terrible things in life.

Amanda came to the end of the performance and the crowd erupted. Looking totally surprised by the response, she stood up and gave a sheepish bow. She looked over at Nathaniel and Vanessa, who of course were on their feet and applauding their little girl.

Nathaniel clapped and whistled and hollered. It was totally out of character for him, but he was so proud, so full of love for his little girl. This was his victory party, he had saved her. He was celebrating the end of his mission – he was just the only one who knew it.

Amanda gave another bow, then giggled as she ran off the stage.

The applause dissipated, and as Vanessa turned to look at Nathaniel, a strange look came over her face.

"What's wrong?" Nathaniel asked.

Without speaking, Vanessa slowly reached over and put her hands either side of his face. He thought in spite of himself that she might be about to kiss him, and he found himself not quite knowing how he was supposed to feel.

A moment later, he felt Vanessa's thumbs gently brush his cheeks, and realised she was wiping away tears from his face.

He hadn't even realised he'd been crying.

"She did very well, didn't she?" Vanessa asked tenderly.

"She did," Nathaniel said. "I knew she would. My Princess Amanda."

Vanessa smiled and went to say something, but stopped herself and gave a brief nod instead.

They held eye contact for just longer than was necessary, and Nathaniel gave a smile. He was sure that Vanessa smiled back too.

They sat back down and a few of the other audience members looked over and commented as to how well Amanda had done. Nathaniel noticed most of the praise was directed towards Vanessa, but he didn't mind. Amanda's performance had gone perfectly, and she was safe. Not just safe, but her daddy had stepped up when he needed to and protected her. Vanessa seemed to have forgiven him too.

Life was good.

For now.

Chapter 33

There were only a couple more performances after Amanda, which was fortunate because Nathaniel wasn't sure how much longer he could wait to see his little girl. He had the same sensation he used to have as a child on Christmas Eve – knowing the big day would come, but feeling as though every second lasted an hour.

He looked around at the audience. They had no idea what was out there, in the real world. The pain and suffering, the existential crises just waiting to break into their safe, cosseted lives.

It's easy to forget the world is on fire when you can't see the flames or smell the smoke.

It was like hearing a noise in the middle of the night, and, instead of going to confront who or whatever may be in the house, you pull the covers over your head. We block things out, because if we can't see them, they don't exist. It was Gary all over again. If everyone turns away from the horrors of the world, maybe they don't exist anymore. Maybe they disappear.

Except Nathaniel knew that they didn't. Everybody knew, really.

But they still looked away. They just developed ways to not notice the smell of smoke anymore.

Nathaniel hadn't, he'd confronted it head on. He'd walked into the inferno and made it back out again.

The end of the concert was announced, and all the performers came onto the stage together and took a bow. Several bows, in fact, as the applause went on for some time. He so desperately wanted to see his little girl and hug her. It was his reward, he'd earned it.

The schoolchildren smiled and accepted the applause in wildly different ways. Some did ironic air kisses to the crowd, others sincere air kisses, while others – Amanda included – looked embarrassed to even still be on stage and getting attention. Nathaniel always found something endearing in that. Not just in Amanda, but in Vanessa too. There was something about modesty, about humility, that made him feel protective. It made him want to hug them and tell them that they were good enough, that there was no need for them to feel as though they didn't match up.

The schoolchildren stepped off stage and the heavy curtain swished across. The show was definitely over now. Nathaniel and Vanessa stood up and began walking to the classroom behind the hall, which was being used as the dressing room.

There was a huge crowd of parents all going the same direction. Nathaniel wondered how they were ever going to plough through to get to Amanda.

They patiently trudged along as the crowd inched forward. Nathaniel was so excited to be seeing his daughter. Nothing else seemed to matter.

He might have felt differently if he had known two police officers had pulled up outside the school. If he had known that the show wasn't quite as over as he'd thought.

***

As they made their way to the classroom-dressing room, Nathaniel noticed Vanessa tensing, then starting to speak to him and stopping herself a couple of times.

"I'm sorry," she suddenly blurted. "OK? I was just worried sick when I heard about the fire, even though there was no reason... no need for me to be worried at all, let alone so over the top about it. I was just asking you about it, and then you were short with me, and... but then you were crying looking at Amanda, and I know you're a good father Nathan, I know you are. It's not that. It's how we are now. Does that make sense? We're not the same. Anyway, no... I didn't want to say all that. Just... sorry. That's all. Sorry for snapping at you before."

Nathaniel saw something he didn't remember ever seeing in Vanessa's face. She seemed confused about how she felt about him. Not confused about what emotion she felt, but confused that the emotion she felt didn't match what she *wanted* to feel.

Nathaniel was right – she still loved him, but didn't want to.

It was reassuring and terrifying in equal measure.

"Vanessa," he said quietly. "Why don't you want to love me anymore?"

At that moment, he saw it in her eyes. Almost an amazement. A realisation that Nathan – her husband – did know her, did understand her. But at the same time, he saw it was yet another source of conflict for her. Yet another tick on the mental scorecard she was keeping, another pro. There needed to be more Xs, more cons.

She looked at him, as if pondering the question for the first time ever.

"I don't know, Nathan," she said sadly. "I just know that I don't."

Nathaniel found he couldn't maintain eye contact anymore. He turned his head to the back of the hall, as if the exit might somehow be a way out not just of the premises, but of the way he was feeling.

He turned just in time to see two police officers milling around just outside the door, scanning the crowds as though looking for someone.

Nathaniel's stomach dropped and he quickly turned around. He didn't want to look at Vanessa, but he certainly didn't want to be spotted by the police. He closed his eyes and wished Aurora would tell him what to do. Or at least put a hand on his shoulder.

They kept walking and, after what felt like an hour, finally reached the dressing room. Nathaniel saw Amanda sitting with her friends. She saw her parents walk in and her face once again lit up.

"Mum! Dad!" she cried, running over to them. Reaching Nathaniel first, she launched herself at him and nearly knocked him backwards. She gave him a hug and he hugged her back, squeezing his beautiful daughter and kissing the top of her head. He felt a lump in his throat, and tried in vain to swallow it down so as not to embarrass Amanda.

"You were *amazing*, Princess Amanda!" he said.

"Thanks, Dad. I'm so glad you came!"

"Of course I came! Nothing was going to stop me getting here!"

He gave Vanessa a glance, wondering what she had said to make Amanda think he might not turn up. It jarred, but he let it go. He didn't want anything to spoil these moments.

"So what did you think of it, Dad? I thought I might mess up that second bit, but I think it went alright."

"It was perfect," he said, meaning it, "absolutely perfect."

"You were brilliant," Vanessa said, stepping forward slightly and embracing Amanda.

"Thanks, Mum!"

"So," Nathaniel said, "is anyone hungry? I know a good place that does all day breakfasts that I think a certain person quite likes going to…"

"Yeah!" said Amanda. "Can we, Mum?"

She looked over at Vanessa, who apparently had the final say. Again, it jarred with Nathaniel, and this time he did say something.

"Of course we can, princess!" Nathaniel said, not waiting for Vanessa to respond. "It's a celebration!"

Amanda smiled but, Nathaniel noticed, kept looking at Vanessa. She gave a reluctant smile and a shrug.

"I suppose so," she said, "it just means we won't need a big dinner later."

"Yay!" Amanda said, giving Nathaniel another hug.

They began getting Amanda's things together when Nathaniel noticed one of the teachers coming over. She was flanked by two police officers – one male and one female. Neither of them looked older than about twenty years of age. For a moment Nathaniel almost laughed at the sight. This slight, petit woman looked like an arch-criminal being escorted by two officers who looked as though they were in her class. Not that Nathaniel did laugh – things were far from funny at this point.

"This is Nathaniel Bennett," the teacher said discreetly by way of introducing the officers to Nathaniel.

He forced a smile and tried to stop his legs from shaking.

"Good afternoon, Mr Bennett," the female officer said. "I'm PC Cole and this is PC Wittich. We'd like to ask you a few questions if we may."

Nathaniel felt his heartbeat skyrocket.

"Sure," he said, "w-what is this about please?"

"It's about the fire at your office. We just need to ask you a few questions, if that's alright?"

"About the person you found?"

"Yes. It's quite a… delicate and sensitive matter," PC Wittich said gently, gesturing with his eyes to Amanda. "It'd be really helpful if you could please come with us so we can talk more privately."

"Daddy, what is this about?"

"Nothing, princess, it's… everything is OK."

He turned back to the officers.

"How long will this take? We were about to go out to eat."

"Oh, not long, I expect," PC Wittich said. "We can just talk outside for a few minutes."

Nathaniel nodded, although wasn't convinced at how casual this was sounding.

He leaned slightly towards the officers. "Could I please have one second to say goodbye to my daughter?"

The two officers looked at each other as if telepathically conferring. Nathaniel got the feeling that PC Wittich was more inclined to give him this moment than PC Cole, who hesitated and gave her colleague a quizzical look.

PC Wittich gave a slight nod.

"Yes," PC Cole said. "If you could please be quick though, Mr Bennett. As my colleague said, if everything is in order then we shouldn't be long and you should be free to go."

Nathaniel paused. That wasn't what her colleague had said at all.

"Of course," he said cautiously, suddenly thinking he should be mindful about the exact wording he used. "Thank you."

Nathaniel crouched down so he was at eye level with Amanda. Somewhere deep down, he could hardly believe things had got to this point. Had he really thought he'd walk away?

Somewhere in his mind he realised that he had. He'd pinned his hopes on Aurora coming through for him, and that hope was still alive somewhere.

"Princess," he said, not quite knowing how to continue. What could he say to her that she would remember? These might be his last words to her. What would encapsulate his love for his daughter?

Could *anything*?

"I love you," he said, feeling tears prick his eyes. "And I'm proud of you. I'm so, so proud, princess. You did so well today, but even if you hadn't, I'd be proud. Do you understand? I love you and I'm proud of you. And that will always be true. OK?"

"OK," she said with a puzzled look.

"Nathan," Vanessa said, "what's going on?"

Nathaniel kept his focus on Amanda. She had to know these things. If this was going to be her last memory of him outside of a jail cell, he needed to make this count. She needed to not just hear him, but understand.

"I love you and I'm proud of you, princess. Say it."

"Daddy…"

He felt a tear roll down one of his cheeks and quickly wiped it away.

"No, no, it's OK baby, just say it. Please. Just say it. I love you."

"You love me."

"And I'm proud of you."

"And you're…" She glanced behind Nathaniel at the police officer."

"It's OK princess. Just look at me. Don't look at them, just me. And I'm proud of you."

"And you're proud of me."

"And that will always be true, princess."

She looked up at Vanessa.

"Nathan," Vanessa said, "you're scaring her."

"I'm not. Please, princess, please, say it."

"And that will always be true."

He leaned forward and hugged her, feeling her tiny body tremble as she began to cry.

"Don't cry, princess," he whispered gently. "Daddy's here. I'll always be here."

"Mr Bennett," PC Cole said. "We really have to go now."

He ignored the statement. He couldn't leave now. He rubbed Amanda's back and gave her a kiss on the cheek.

"It's OK, princess. It's OK."

"Mr Bennett?" The tone of PC Cole was getting increasingly impatient.

All of a sudden, he felt the tears flow uncontrollably down his face, as the consequences of all he'd done bore down on him. He had done this – all of this – for Amanda. Would this really be their last embrace?

He felt a hand on his shoulder as one of the officers began gently but firmly pulling him away.

Vanessa crouched down, and tried to pry her husband's hands away from Amanda.

He didn't want to let go. He *couldn't*. What if he never had this opportunity again?

"Please let go, Nathan," Vanessa said. "You're scaring her."

"What are you doing, Daddy?"

"I love you, princess."

He leaned back from the embrace and grabbed Amanda's shoulders.

"You're safe from harm," he said urgently into her face. "You're safe. I did it for you. You have to understand."

"Nathan! Let her go!" Vanessa shouted.

He felt one of the officers yank his shoulder, and the other one pulling him from the other side.

"Mr Bennett, please let go of her."

He looked at his daughter's face and suddenly realised she was afraid. He let go of her immediately and she turned and wept into her mother's side.

"No, it's OK, Princess Amanda. It's me, Daddy. Don't be scared," he called as the officers led him away. "I love you and I'm proud of you. I love you and I'm proud of you. Everybody loves Princess Amanda. Why, princess? Why does everybody love Princess Amanda? Please! Say it! Because Princess Amanda is…? Say it, my beautiful girl. I'm begging you."

The police took him out of the room, and for a single, terrible-but-beautiful moment, he thought he heard his daughter's voice say a single word.

Lovely.

Chapter 34

The police officers led Nathaniel outside the classroom, down the corridor and out of a fire exit. They stood in the playground opposite the car park, Nathaniel noticed. Parents and their happy children walked to their cars, probably planning a late lunch or early dinner just like he had been.

He's saved them. He needed to hold onto that, no matter what. Just like Aurora had said.

"Sir, I think we should just take a moment and calm down," PC Wittich said. "Let's just try to relax. I don't want to handcuff you, and at the moment there's no need, so let's just try and keep it that way. How does that sound?"

Nathaniel nodded. His shoulders jerked as he tried to stop his sobs.

"It sounds good," he said.

The three of them stood together looking like a bunch of friends waiting for a fourth to join. Nathaniel knew that wasn't the case though, and he also knew it wouldn't really look like that to any onlookers either. It was two against one, and even if it had only been one on one, that *one* would still be the *police*. The power imbalance was massive.

Nathaniel tried to keep calm and focus his mind. What should he be doing? If Aurora was here, what would she tell him? Probably to breathe and try to relax, maybe to focus on his mission. Although his mission was over now, wasn't it? The only thing left to focus on was survival.

But what did that mean? Keep quiet? Cooperate with the police?

A thought suddenly occurred to him.

"Am I under arrest?" he asked, immediately regretting the question. Innocent people didn't ask if they were being arrested, surely. He couldn't believe this was a sentence he was actually uttering, it was like a scene in an action film.

PC Wittich was the one to speak again.

"No, sir, you are not under arrest. We would like to speak with you about the fire at your office and the circumstances surrounding it. As I said, you're not under arrest, and it will also not be an interview under caution. We just need to ask you some questions. Does that sound agreeable to you?"

Nathaniel hesitated. Not much sounded agreeable at this point. He kept seeing Amanda's scared face, the feel of her little body tensing up as he tried to keep hold of her.

After all he'd been through for her, was that going to outweigh everything else he'd done?

"Do you think she'll forgive me?" he asked.

"Who is that, sir?" PC Cole asked.

"My daughter. In there. Do you think she'll forgive me."

PC Cole looked at PC Wittich as if deferring the question to him, apparently aware that he was the more empathetic one.

"I can't say," he said gently. "I do know that children are very resilient and as long as a parent is loving and has their best intentions at heart, they're likely to forgive mistakes here and there."

"Mistakes?"

"Yes, sir."

"What kind of mistakes?"

"Well, that depends, Mr Bennett," PC Cole jumped in before PC Wittich could respond. "What kind of mistakes are we talking about exactly?"

He looked at the two officers, and in a second he knew that both now suspected him. And not just for the fire. If a body was intact enough to be found then surely the bullets inside that body would be too. Although he'd got the gun from the dark web, Aurora had directed him. There was no link to Nathaniel. Although what links did the police

need? What did they have access to? They were the *police*.
The word kept flashing into his mind in flashing blue neon.
He had no idea what forensic science they could use, what
techniques to look for fingerprints or DNA, or who knew
whatever else. He literally didn't know, what he didn't know
about a criminal investigation.

The reality of his situation hit Nathaniel square in
the face. He couldn't outmanoeuvre the police. He was a
manager at an office supply company. He had a full-time
job, a mortgage, a failing marriage, a child. He wasn't a
criminal mastermind. He was an average man in an insane
situation.

He also knew there was only one direction this was
all headed.

"Mr Bennett? You were saying something about
mistakes. I was just asking what you were referring to."

"Things that can't be undone," he said, staring into
the distance. "Although things that needed to be done."

He felt tears roll down his cheeks and choked on his
words as he spoke again.

"Things that I wish I didn't have to do, but that
nobody else could."

PC Wittich spoke again.

"Mr Bennett, maybe we shou—"

"They were going to kill the children. What could I do? What would you do?"

The officers were silent, not as though they were weighing up the question, but as though waiting for Nathaniel to say more.

"The question is," PC Cole finally said, "what *did* you do, sir?"

Nathaniel looked up, his eyes burning as the tears flowed relentlessly.

"I k-killed them. I killed all three of them. And I can tell you when and where and how. They were going to kill my daughter, I swear. My daughter! Aurora showed me, she showed me everything."

"I don't know who Aurora is, Mr Bennett, but we're at the point where we need to discuss this at the police station. I must also now advise you that you *are* now under arrest. You do not have to say anything, but it may harm your defence if you do not mention when questioned something which you later rely on in court. Anything you do say may be given in evidence. Do you understand, sir?"

"Yes. I understand."

PC Cole took out handcuffs but was stopped by the look on PC Wittich's face.

"Are handcuffs going to be necessary?" PC Wittich asked carefully.

"That depends," PC Cole replied, looking at Nathaniel. "Are these going to be necessary, sir?"

Nathaniel – weary, beaten and with no fight left in him – shook his head. The air felt thick around him, heavy. It was as though he was moving underwater.

PC Cole put away her handcuffs, and Nathaniel was led over to the police car. It was only a few steps away, but the walk felt like a long one.

As they guided him into the back of the car he watched as the parents filed out with their kids, and stared in horror as he saw Vanessa coming out with Amanda. Vanessa saw him, froze, and then quickly spun Amanda to face the opposite direction so she wouldn't see him.

That's when something inside him snapped. If this was the last time his little girl was going to see him, it wouldn't be in the back of a police car being led away like a criminal. He was a hero. He'd saved her, he'd saved them all.

With strength and agility he didn't know he had in his body, he launched himself out of the police car and ran in the direction of his own vehicle. There was no plan outside of that – he just needed to get to his car and get away from all this.

The adrenalin coursed through him, and he suddenly felt like he was in a computer game. The people he dodged, the other vehicles, all of them may as well have been pixels on a screen. They didn't matter. He had a new mission now.

Escape.

He thought he vaguely heard voices behind him – incomprehensible shouts, possibly someone calling his name – but none of it meant anything.

He turned a corner and zeroed in what looked like the roof of his car. As he ran he reached into his pocket and grabbed his keys, frantically pressing the 'unlock' button on the key fob so it'd open as soon as he was in range.

More pixels appeared in his way, but he deftly swerved and slipped them like a boxer dodging punches. His legs burned but it didn't matter. His focus was on his new mission.

He had the vague sense of more shouts and then suddenly felt a huge force impact his right side. He found himself flying through the air, sideways. The breath knocked out of him, he had the strange sensation of feeling both weightless and incredibly heavy. As if he were on a roller-coaster, being pushed unnaturally in an impossible direction at the highest of speeds.

In the seconds before he hit the ground, he realised two things.

He'd been hit by a car.

This might be Amanda's last image of him.

Chapter 35

Nathaniel awoke in a hospital bed. The first thing he noticed was the searing pain in the right-side of his body. It felt as though he'd been put into a vice and mercilessly crushed.

He looked around the room, forcing his eyes to focus so he could take stock of the situation. He realised he was by himself, not on a ward. He wasn't hooked up to a drip or anything. He also didn't feel particularly disorientated, so concluded two things.

Firstly, he must not be too badly hurt. But secondly, they'd probably put him in his own room so he wouldn't try to escape again. The gravity of that struck him hard.

He looked down towards his hands, instinctively raising them both to ensure he wasn't handcuffed to the bed.

The memory of the car park came back to him in full – the police, the chase, the vehicle slamming into him. He hoped Amanda hadn't seen any of it. What an image that would be for her young mind to process.

A nurse entered the room. He was a heavyset man, looking more like a bouncer than a carer. Nathaniel wondered if he was a nurse at all, or a member of law enforcement working undercover.

Or maybe this was some kind of special hospital for suspected criminals?

"You'll be alright, Nathan. You'll be alright. Doctor Gallo will be in to see you shortly," he said with a strange look in his eyes that Nathaniel couldn't identify.

"How long have I been here? Am I badly injured?" Nathaniel asked. His throat felt dry and he wondered whether there was any water around.

"You got a very nasty hit from the car. You haven't been here long. The doctor isn't a medical doctor, by the way. She is a… different kind of doctor," the nurse replied.

"What other type of…"

Nathaniel trailed off as he identified the look in the nurse's eyes. Pity, shot through with apprehension.

Nathaniel had seen that look before. Years ago a colleague had a nervous breakdown and taken a long leave of absence. After four months, he was phased back into the office, first part-time then slowly building up to full-time again. Nathaniel had been appointed his 'buddy' to help him settle back into things. In the first week, without exception, every single person who had come up to welcome him back had the same look on their face. Pity, apprehension. Sad for his problems, but terrified about what this 'insane' person might do to them.

The nurse felt sorry for Nathaniel, but also feared him.

Seeing that same look in the eyes of the nurse, Nathaniel knew that this doctor would be a specialist in either psychiatry or psychology. They were going to assess him. Probably mere minutes before the police came in to interrogate him.

***

Not long after, the doctor arrived.

Nathaniel had been expecting an old man with a white beard and little round glasses perched on the bridge of his nose. He imagined bushy eyebrows, and fat temples run through with indentations where the arms of his glasses would have dug in over the years.

Instead, a woman who seemed to be in her late thirties walked in. She had jet black hair cut into a bob, and Nathaniel noticed a thumb ring on one hand and three more rings on the other. She was dressed fairly casually, although not scruffy. She'd obviously put thought into the clothes, she just hadn't seen the need to wear particularly formal attire.

When she spoke, Nathaniel detected a slight accent, possibly Italian.

"Mr Bennett," she said warmly, and gave what looked to Nathaniel to be a genuine smile. "I am Doctor Marcella Gallo. How are you feeling?"

"I'm feeling... fairly well."

"That's good. I'm here to have a chat with you. Does that sound OK?"

Nathaniel searched her face for any sign of pretence. If she was faking sincerity, she was very good at it.

"Yes," he said, "it sounds fine."

"Great," she said, her smile not fading for a second.

She sat on the small plastic chair by Nathaniel's bed. It had seen better days, but then so had he.

"Now," the doctor continued, "just so you know, I'm not a police officer or a lawyer or anything like that. That means that I cannot give legal advice and I'm also not here to trick you or trip you up. My job is just to talk to you. That's it. Let's just chat for a while."

"I understand."

"Great," she said again, as if he'd just asked how her holiday had been. "Now from what I understand, you were in a rather heightened emotional state and made some sort of confession to the police. Is there anything you'd like to tell me regarding this at all? For instance, whether it was true?"

Nathaniel sighed, and wondered what Aurora would want him to say. Surely at this point, arrested and knocked down by a car or some other vehicle while running from the police, the game was over. Lying at this point would get him into even more trouble. Although he wasn't sure that was even possible now. He'd already confessed to the police anyway. He was tired, surely it was time to confess and get it over with?

"Those men that I…" He couldn't find the right formulation of words that wouldn't make him look delusional. He'd decided to tell the doctor everything, but now found himself unable to.

"Sorry," he said, "this is… what sort of doctor are you? I don't mean that in a rude way, I just mean, have you dealt with stories that may not sound completely… of this world?"

"I have been doing this job for so long now I've lost count of the years," she said good naturedly. "I'm not often surprised. Please don't worry about that though. The important thing here is you. The focus isn't on me, it's on you and how you feel and what you can tell me. Like I said, I'm not a police officer or a lawyer or any of those things. I'm not here to judge you. Just to listen."

Something about her reminded Nathaniel of Aurora, although not in the same way. Where Aurora calmed him with her very presence, this doctor had the same effect merely through her words.

"The men that I told the officers about," he continued, "they were going to do bad things. Really bad things. They were going to kill children."

The doctor frowned.

"And you stopped them?" she asked gently.

"Yes."

"So if you hadn't done what you did, then…"

"Then they were going to detonate bombs in schools and kill hundreds of innocent children. And that was going to lead to…"

He suddenly felt ridiculous.

"Please, go on," she said.

He looked in her face for some sign of doubt or amusement. There was none. She was very good at this.

"It was going to lead to riots and more campaigns from other people. So deaths, leading to more deaths, and then even more deaths. The whole planet would get involved one way or another."

"So, in a sense, you feel that you saved the world?"

He closed his eyes and debated stopping this whole thing. But what harm could it do now? If she was going to call him a liar or a crazy person, then surely she would've done it already.

"Yes, I think so. I was led to believe so."

"OK. Can I ask you, how did you know that these events were going to happen? The bombings and then the other attacks and so on? Did you see plans?"

"No. I mean, I was shown the explosions and the aftermath of it all. I was taken to the sites of the bombings and saw them happen."

"In the future?"

"Yes. Look, I know how this sounds, but it's true. I know I sound deluded but I'm not. Please believe me. These things were going to happen. They were going to kill my daughter. What could I do?"

The doctor opened a file and scanned the contents for a moment.

"Your daughter… and that's Amanda?"

"Yes, that's right."

"So, you undertook all this in order to save her? Knowing that you may well end up in prison for the rest of your life?"

He sighed.

"What father wouldn't do the same? My life for my Princess Amanda's. I can survive a prison cell if I know she's out there living and healthy and happy. My life is less important than hers."

"And what if one of these men, these potential killers, killed you first? Did you think at all about your own well-being, about possibly not surviving this? To me, pursuing three dangerous men like this could quite easily end up with them walking away and you ending up—"

Her phone rang, and she abruptly stopped talking. It was an odd sound, Nathaniel noticed, more like a siren than a ringtone. What kind of person would have a siren noise for a ringtone? Maybe this doctor was more 'medical' than she had first appeared.

"Sorry, I have to get this," she said, answering the call and bringing the phone to her ear in one smooth movement.

"Yes?" she said in a tone which managed to be both professional yet somehow friendly. "Mm-hmm. Alright. I'll be there soon. Stay with her if you can."

She ended the call.

"Sorry about that. As I was saying, what if you ended up—"

"—in hospital? As you can see, that's where I *have* ended up. But it doesn't matter. If they killed me, as long as Amanda was safe, it wouldn't matter. We're all going to die, doctor. It's inevitable. It's not about that, it's about how we've lived. Did we help? Did we love? Were we loved? And if I now spend the rest of my life in a cell, again, it doesn't matter. I still did the right thing. I'm certain of it."

The doctor nodded her head solemnly.

"And what about the fact that they hadn't yet done anything? In a sense, the argument could be made that you didn't kill three bombers – they hadn't bombed anyone yet. So, who did you kill?"

"Those men were going to do horrific things…"

"I know, and let's say you could know for sure, that without a doubt, they were going to go on and do these things. They hadn't yet done them, had they? How will a jury look at that do you think?"

He paused and thought for a moment. Her tone was still kind, and he didn't feel she was challenging him, it did feel more like a chat. In fact, he wondered if he was being lulled into a false sense of security. Not that it would make much difference now anyway.

"I don't think… The focus isn't on a jury, it's on Amanda and those other kids. If you could prevent a massacre, and you didn't, how would you live with yourself? A jury judging me is one thing, but not taking action and judging myself for those deaths would be too much. I probably shouldn't say this, but I'm proud of what I did. I am. This was the purpose of my life and I've fulfilled it."

Something changed in her demeanour then. It was as though he'd finally given the answer she had been looking for.

"Is that how you feel? That you fulfilled the purpose of your life? That you have achieved what you were put on this earth to do?"

He paused again, although for a much shorter time.

"Yes," he said definitively, "I do."

"I'm glad to hear that, Nathaniel. And I agree. I think you've successfully achieved the purpose of your life. You stopped those men, you saved Amanda, you saved millions – one way or another. And, as you said, we're all going to die, aren't we? It's about how we lived."

She stood up and walked over to him.

She took his hand and stared intently at him.

"Are you at peace with your decisions, Nathaniel?" she asked gently. "Do you feel that, no matter the consequences, it was worth doing what you did? Could you die happy now?"

He looked at her, trying to read her expression. She didn't look dangerous, although he suddenly wondered if she wasn't a doctor at all, but was there to avenge one of the men. Was this a trap?

He wondered if he should've said anything at all.

Her face was kind though, radiating a genuine concern for him.

"It's not what you think, Nathaniel," he heard Aurora say from the corner of the room. "She's not dangerous."

He looked over at her, and felt relief and an immense calmness pulse through his body. It was more intense and more total than any calmness he had ever felt. It wasn't the same sensation he'd have whenever Aurora would appear, it was more intense. It didn't just calm him in that moment, it seemingly went back and undid every negative emotion he'd ever felt. It undid all the bad that had been done. He smiled.

He looked back at the doctor, and this time successfully read her expression. He looked over at Aurora by way of confirmation.

She nodded.

For the first time, Nathaniel understood. He understood it all.

This wasn't a hospital. This woman wasn't a doctor. He was safe now.

"I really did it, didn't I, Aurora? My Princess Amanda."

"Yes," Aurora said. "You did it, Nathaniel."

He closed his eyes. The fight was over.

"I love you and I'm sorry, Vanessa," he said. "I love you, Amanda. I love you and I'm proud of you, and that will always be true."

Chapter 36

Life is confusing.

In any given life, at any given time, there are too many things to think about all at once. Going to work, looking after the kids, maintaining relationships and friendships, cooking, cleaning, and the million other things needed to keep 'life' going. It's a constant juggling act.

Tragedy is the opposite.

Tragedy *focuses*.

It cuts through the bullshit and the drama and the nonsense of everyday life and shows people what matters. It says *this* is what is important, *this* is what you should be focusing on.

The argument a person has with their partner pales into insignificance the moment one of them slices the tip of their finger off while chopping vegetables. The irritation of having to visit elderly relatives quickly turns to a yearning for that very inconvenience after they die.

That's how it was when, after rushing towards the squeal of brakes and a horrific thud, Vanessa saw Nathan's crumpled body lying in front of a car. Her mind focused on him, and nobody and nothing else. Worrying about him in that fire suddenly seemed like a trial run for the real thing.

She'd never heard the sound of a body being hit by a car, but it was one of those sounds that couldn't be mistaken for much else. The sound of a soft object with a solid core being impacted by a huge metal machine.

Mercifully, Amanda hadn't witnessed anything. After seeing Nathan with the police, Vanessa had quickly bundled her into the car. She was safely strapped into her car seat with her favourite book and the door firmly closed.

In an instinctive gesture, Vanessa rushed over to Nathan and crouched beside him. He lay on his right-side, almost in the foetal position, and blood was quickly pooling beneath him. The dark grey of the playground around him began turning a deep, rich crimson.

His breath was ragged, and Vanessa heard a vague gurgling sound every time he breathed.

She stroked his hair, afraid to touch anywhere else in case she did any more damage. Tears flowed from her eyes as she looked at his broken and bloodied form.

"I'm here, Nathan," she said, "It's me. Vanessa."

His hand twitched slightly at the sound of her voice, and he slowly opened and closed it a few times. She carefully placed her hand inside his. He hesitated for a moment, then closed his hand around hers. He squeezed tight this time and didn't open his hand again.

"I won't let go, Nathan," she said.

There was a commotion around her but she barely registered. Her mind was in tragedy mode, her focus fixed on her husband. She was vaguely aware that people were screaming and talking about ambulances. At one point, she saw figures wearing uniforms in her peripheral vision – probably the same police officers she had seen earlier with Nathan although she didn't know or care.

One of the uniformed figures carefully reached over and placed two fingers on Nathaniel's neck, feeling around for his carotid artery. He then called numbers into a radio, adding the words "need them here now!" in a frantic tone.

"Nathan," the figure said. "Can you hear me?"

He stirred again slightly at the mention of his name. He kept his grip tight on Vanessa's hand, as if she were somehow anchoring him.

"You'll be alright, Nathan. You'll be alright."

Vanessa looked over and recognised the officer. She saw the expression on his face and knew he wasn't convinced of his own words.

Nathaniel mumbled, and Vanessa thought she picked up the words 'doctor' and 'injured'.

"You got a very nasty hit from the car," the officer continued.

Vanessa stroked her husband's hair again, and noticed his eyes were closed but flickering behind his eyelids. His whole body seemed to be veering between twitching and moving one moment, and then totally still the next. Vanessa felt herself fear that at some point he would go still and never start moving again.

"Nathan," Vanessa said gently. "I'm here, Nathan. Let's just chat for a while."

He started moving again, but she wasn't sure if he was stirring at the sound of her voice, or just trying to shift position.

He winced and took a sharp intake of breath, causing him to cough. Vanessa suddenly realised his breaths were not only irregular, but were sounding wetter than before. Not as if he was choking, but almost as though the slight gurgling sound at the beginning and end of each breath was getting worse. As though the fluid had got somehow deeper.

"Try not to move, Nathan," she said.

He took a deep breath and said something but Vanessa couldn't make it out. She leaned closer in an attempt to block out the background hum of the crowd that had gathered around them.

"What's that, Nathan?"

"Bombs…"

She glanced up at the police officer to see if he was hearing the same thing, but he was facing the other way. It looked as though he was scanning the road, most likely for any sign of an ambulance.

"Kill hundreds…"

Vanessa stiffened at her husband's words.

"Nathan… what are you saying? It isn't making any sense."

"My life for Princess Amanda's…."

"No! What do you mean? Stay with us, Nathan. Stay with me and Amanda. Both your lives, Nathan. I want both!"

Vanessa heard a siren in the distance, and hoped the ambulance was on its way. She felt a hand on her shoulder and turned to see one of the other mothers from Amanda's class.

"Is Amanda in the car?" she asked. "Shall I go and check on her?"

"Yes, please," Vanessa said, still trying to piece together what Nathan was saying. "I'll be there soon. Stay with her if you can."

The woman gave Vanessa's shoulder a squeeze and rushed away. Vanessa turned her attention back to Nathan.

"As long as Amanda… safe."

"She is, Nathan. We're all safe. You just focus on getting into that ambulance. It's coming soon. That was Kaylin's mum, Kimberley. You remember her? She said she's going to stay with Amanda."

She stared at him, watching the staccato breaths coming from his battered body. She realised the blood that had seeped from his right-side had pooled so much that it was now touching her shoes. She wondered if she was seeing his life literally spilling out of him.

She wasn't sure how much of him was even still there.

The police officer put his hand on Nathaniel's neck again, waited a few moments, then looked over at his colleague. He gave a short, but undeniable shake of his head.

"His pulse is getting weaker," he said, then – turning to Vanessa – "keep talking to him. He seems to be responding to your voice."

In that moment Vanessa felt both an overwhelming panic alongside an overwhelming sense of responsibility. She couldn't collapse, not now. Nathan needed her. Her voice might be the only recognisable thing he could cling to.

"Just think about Amanda, Nathan," she said. "Princess Amanda. I know we've had our problems,

Nathan, and all marriages do. Children are the purpose of it all, aren't they? She needs you, Nathan. I... I need you."

Fresh tears rolled down her cheeks, creating hot rivulets down her cold face.

"We love you, Nathan. Stay with us. I'm so sorry for everything that's happened between us. I love you. Please, Nathan."

An odd thing happened then. Nathaniel's breathing settled, and his grip on her hand relaxed slightly. It was as if he had somehow calmed. His chest moved up and down rhythmically. No more ragged breaths. No more gurgling.

She felt her husband's fingers caress the back of her hand in the most bittersweet sensation she had ever felt.

She looked at his face and, incredibly, he was smiling. His eyes were open, and he was staring somewhere into the middle distance. His eyes glazed, seemingly unfixed on anything.

"I really did it, didn't I, Aurora? My Princess Amanda."

He closed his eyes.

"I love you and I'm sorry, Vanessa. I love you, Amanda. I love you and I'm proud of you, and that will always be true."

And with that, Nathaniel Bennett took his last breath. His mission was over.

Chapter 37

After the concert had ended, so did Amanda's piano playing.

Vanessa had tried encouraging her, thinking it might help her through the pain she'd inevitably be feeling. Nothing seemed to work. Vanessa didn't blame her. She needed time to grieve. That was the thing with bereavement, there is no shortcut. The pain can't be avoided, it shouldn't be either. It's part of the process. It has to be endured. Otherwise a person gets stuck in the middle somewhere and gets lost in the searing agony of loss.

Not that Vanessa was feeling much better than Amanda. She was grieving too, spending hours sitting on the sofa she and Nathan had shared for so many years, staring blankly at whatever was on television to feel less alone.

Shay had been round, and made frequent phone calls. She also sent messages to Vanessa's phone – some heartfelt, some funny, some just a reassuring *I'm here*. It helped, but of course nothing could replace the person Vanessa had lost.

And on top of that, she was trying to piece together just what type of man Nathaniel Bennett had been. The police had grilled her for hours, trying to find out what she knew about the murders – the *murders!* – that her husband had apparently committed. The Nathan she knew needed routine, structure, he wasn't a killer.

But then, according to the evidence, he was.

All she had to explain his actions were the words he had said to the police officers, and the words he had said to her as he lay dying. He spoke about bombs being detonated, and hundreds of people dying. It made no sense to her.

The media were having a field day. They loved the family-man-turns-out-to-be-a-serial-killer angle. Not to mention the way he'd died, in a school playground surrounded by shocked families who'd never known him as anything but one of them. The glee with which they wrote about him, and quoted so called 'friends' sickened Vanessa to her very core.

They were almost disappointed that Nathan hadn't started the fire in his office. The investigation turned up a faulty fuse as the cause, which swept through the offices and the various products in the warehouse relentlessly. Being an office supply company meant an abundance of paper, cardboard, and various cleaning products in aerosol cans. Alongside the old, dangerously flammable upholstery of the office chairs, it had been a recipe for disaster since before Nathan even started working there. Not that some of the sections of the media hadn't taken the opportunity to imply that Nathan had somehow deliberately not stored items correctly. They had the story they wanted to write in their heads, the facts weren't about to stop them.

Vanessa acknowledged that she may not have known exactly who Nathan was, but she couldn't accept him as a killer. A serial killer, no less. That wasn't him. She'd never accept that story. No matter what the apparent evidence – or wild conjecture – that was presented to her.

She sat on the sofa with Amanda, who slept soundly next to her mum. Every so often Vanessa reached over and stroked the side of the sofa where Nathan used to sit. The absence of him was almost as tangible as his presence. She didn't know – would never know – how he himself had that very thought about her while lying in his lonely bed.

She thought about their last exchange as she had stroked his head in the playground. Had he known she was there? She hoped so. She felt as though she'd been a failure as his wife, the very least she could have done was made his last moments peaceful.

She lay back on the sofa and closed her eyes. She took a few deep breaths and tried to forget the sound of Nathan's ragged, wet breathing.

Moments later, she opened her eyes and sat bolt upright, nearly waking Amanda.

Vanessa didn't believe in a sixth sense, but suddenly felt a curious sensation. It was as though her being had detected something it had never detected before. Like a baby feeling a sudden change in temperature for the first time, or a person witnessing some miraculous or inexplicable event. Something was happening, something huge and unprecedented, but she had no idea what.

Her eyes darted around the room, but nothing seemed amiss.

Curiously, the overriding sensation was calmness. She felt loved and protected and as though the world existed *around* her without being able to touch her. She didn't even miss Nathan anymore. She was aware of the sensation of grief, but it was over there now. Somewhere else. Behind glass where it couldn't quite get to her.

She felt her eyes drawn back to the end of the room and now saw a figure standing, almost hovering. She didn't know how, but she knew that the source of all the good that she was feeling emanated from this figure.

"Vanessa. Amanda," the figure said gently.

Amanda stirred and Vanessa nodded. Tears began to flow from their eyes.

"My name is Aurora. Everything that Nathaniel – that your daddy – said was true. I'd like to tell you just what a hero he was and what he did for you. What he did for the world."

Aurora spoke. Vanessa and Amanda listened.

***

An hour later, while Vanessa was upstairs, she heard the vague sounds of Amanda playing the piano again. She recognised it immediately – the piece Amanda had composed for the concert. She was note-perfect, Vanessa noticed.

At the end of the piece, Vanessa heard the lid of the piano softly close, and her daughter's small, quiet voice asking herself a question.

"Why does everyone love Princess Amanda?"

Vanessa looked over at the photo of her and Nathan's wedding day.

And for a moment – for the briefest possible time – she swore she heard her husband's voice.

"Because Princess Amanda is lovely."

Dear Reader,

Thank you for reading my fourth novel, Whoever Fights Monsters.

The concept of the story came to me out of nowhere one day, and I just suddenly thought to myself, 'What if a serial killer turned out to be right?'

At the same time, my little boy was born around this time, and I quickly realised that one of the only things that could push the average person to kill would be to protect their family. And so was born the story of Nathaniel Bennett and his Princess Amanda.

Anyway, I hope you enjoyed it. I would love to hear your feedback, so please do get in touch either through my website at **http://www.angelomarcos.com** *or via email at* **info@angelomarcos.com**

Like all independent authors, I greatly appreciate – and, well, need! – reviews, so I'd really appreciate you taking a minute to review the book too.

For a limited time I'm also offering a free short story – **Killing Time** *– to anyone who signs up to my email list. If you're interested take a look here https://killingtimebyangelomarcos.wordpress.com*

Lastly, you might also like my other paranormal thriller Sleep No More, so I've included the first few chapters of it over the page.

Thanks again for reading!

Angelo

Sleep No More by Angelo Marcos

Still it cried "Sleep no more!" to all the house: "Glamis hath murder'd sleep, and therefore Cawdor Shall sleep no more; Macbeth shall sleep no more."

Macbeth (Act 2, Scene 2), William Shakespeare

Prologue

The suit they buried him in was over twenty years old and, up until the funeral, unworn.

It was the first time in years the mourners had been in the man's presence outside a small room thick with the stench of disinfectant, the first time in years that the widow had been able to speak softly to her husband without the rhythmic hiss of the respirator in her ear. Each sentence timed to coincide with one of the brief pauses. The breath of the machine kept his body alive, the widow dared hope her own breath may have had the same effect on his soul.

He'd been dead for only a few days, but had been mourned much longer. It had been two decades since he was robbed of what the newspapers called his 'prime of life'. He had lost everything but his body - a shell of organs and skin, kept alive by machines. A car without an engine, being pushed along in the futile hope that it would one day start again.

The doctors performed tests every so often, the results always communicated with a shake of the head, a consoling look. They spoke about levels of consciousness, and the Glasgow Coma Scale. They tested for eye movement with flashing lights, and pain responses with pinpricks to the feet. They were able to ascertain the exact levels of his non-responsiveness, able to keep him alive with the aid of the best medical equipment available.

In short, they did everything. Except heal him.

His widow watched the coffin – a different type of vehicle now - being slowly lowered into the ground.

The slings and arrows had hit their target, she thought, and they had won.

There was only one remaining truth that gave her any comfort now.

This isn't over.

One

In the deepest recesses of her mind - like an undersea trench impenetrable by light - Ariadne knows she is dreaming. She knows, but it doesn't matter. He is hunting her, and he is going to find her and he is going to hurt her.

Just like he had done every night for the past two weeks.

She stands in the deserted lobby of a plush hotel, her threadbare tracksuit crudely juxtaposed against the lavish surroundings. As she waits for the lift that will take her up to her room, she nervously shifts her weight from one foot to the other. Her gym shoes squeak on the marble floor with every movement but she doesn't care. The cathedral-like interior of the hotel and its smooth, polished surfaces work as a security system to her – the click of footsteps would ricochet around the space, notifying her of the arrival of any other person.

As long as there are no other sounds, she knows she is alone.

The secure feeling is short lived as an uneasiness begins creeping up on her. The shadow form that has been following her is growing closer, she can sense it. The shiver racing through her soul tells her that now she is most definitely not alone. She freezes, unable to do anything but impotently wait for the lift. The vehicle that will take her to safety.

She realises that she heard no footsteps. But then, there are never any footsteps with him.

The being – *he* – is getting closer. She sees the shadow lengthening, his head and shoulders leeching slowly up the wall of the lift doors. She measures his proximity not only through sight but also through the intensity of her fear. As she feels the violation of his hot breath on her neck, the lift arrives and the doors slide open. Immediately, her muscles are freed and she bolts into the metal chamber, finding the strength to turn and face her attacker. A thick shadow form of a man hangs impossibly in the air, his face a blur - always a blur - and always the same. He makes no attempt to move towards her, and stands defiantly watching as the lift doors close.

She begins the ride to safety and notices that the lift is mirrored on all sides. The small spotlight in the ceiling illuminates the tiny space as though it were floodlit. She glimpses her reflection – her tracksuit is gone, replaced now by a long red dress. She begins smoothing her hair and reapplying her lipstick. She isn't going up to her room anymore, instead she is speeding towards the grand roof-top party which has been organised in her honour by the hotel manager.   The fear is a distant memory – an old acquaintance not invited and not considered.

The lift opens and she glides into the room, her elegant gown flowing behind as she flits from one guest to another. Now she sees an old friend, now an ex-boyfriend who cannot stop looking at her. She registers his glances, knowing he still loves her in spite of the woman at his side wearing the wedding ring. A waiter offers her a glass of champagne, which she gratefully accepts, playfully curtseying the young man to the accepting laughter of the crowd. The graceful music of the band swells as she makes her way around the room, gracefully nodding at the other partygoers. The floor-to-ceiling windows give a stunning panorama of the city of London. She is the belle of the ball and this is her city tonight.

The moon illuminates the metropolis spectacularly, the light bouncing off the Houses of Parliament and, farther away, the mighty buildings at Canary Wharf. She saunters over to the glass and peruses the streets below, deserted except for a handful of cars speeding along the back streets. She thinks it must either be very late at night, or very early in the morning.

The hands that violently grab her neck are cold, as though belonging to the undead. She tries to scream, but the pressure on her crushed throat is too great. The champagne flute drops from her hand and she watches as it somehow shatters instead of gently bouncing off the lush carpet. She bangs on the window with her clenched fist, desperately trying to signal for help, and is forcefully whipped around, her attacker now with his - because she knows it is *him* again - back to the window. His form stands defiantly again, this time against the backdrop of the metropolis below. It is his city now.

She twists her neck around and stares pleadingly at the partygoers, who gleefully raise their glasses and toast the spectacle. Red clouds descend over her vision, creeping inwards from the rims of her irises towards her pupils, and her oxygen-starved brain begins the process of shutting down. Her body goes limp and the stranglehold is released. She falls to her knees, her hands on the deep white carpet, her bruised neck barely able to hold up her head.

The crowd smile at her, and she hears the faint noise of an engine from the back of the room. Her eyes are half-closed, but she forces herself to look up toward the direction of the sound. The door is ajar and she sees the edge of a bed. Her gaze fixed on the heavy door, she watches as time slows and a car splinters through, the wood easily shattering like her wineglass an eternity ago. The front of the car now crushes the partygoers, who laugh and smile and dance as they bleed and contort and die in front of her eyes. The entire scene is speeding backwards away from her now, as though the faster the car races toward her, the faster she is being pulled backwards out of harm's way.

He wants to prolong the agony.

She sees that the driver's face is obscured, and registers the inevitability of what is about to happen. Impotently, she raises a hand to stop the vehicle coming towards her. The car does not let up and in a second decimates her hand, arm and shoulder. She is thrown backwards through the window, the glass exploding into a million shards. The car – pulled by gravity now - hurtles with her as she rushes backwards towards the empty street and her inevitable death.

She sees the blackness where the shadow's face should be. There are no features, but she knows he is smiling.

Just before her slight body is burst open by the street and crushed by the car, Ariadne finally – mercifully - wakes up.

***

Ariadne Perasmenos lies motionless in her bed, the duvet on the floor having been kicked off during the night. Her dog lies snuggled amidst the duvet - at least someone made good use of it. She looks blearily at the clock on her bedside table, 5.30am - too early to go to work, too late to go back to sleep. With an almighty effort, she wrenches herself out of bed, the weight of the dream hanging heavy on her shoulders. She walks to the bathroom – quietly so as not to wake the dog - and steps into the shower. She strips quickly and throws her clothes out of the cubicle and onto the tiled floor, wanting to wash the dream away.

The hot water feels good pulsing over her skin. She closes her eyes and allows the pressure to massage her face and shoulders. She runs both hands through her hair, her nails slightly scratching her scalp but reminding her that she is alive. She blindly reaches for the soap, a slight niggling feeling tugging at her, and begins scrubbing at her face, trying to remove any vestige of the dream.

As the water cascades down her body, she suddenly realises that she can taste something rich and metallic. She lets the soap drop onto the shower tray and rinses her face directly under the shower head, trying to get rid of the taste in her throat and stench in her nostrils. The tugging of the negative feeling gets more pronounced, as though she knows she should register what is wrong, but it's escaping her. Just like the car in her dream, the closer she gets to this undiscovered feeling, the farther away she is pulled from it.

She wipes her eyes with the backs of her hands, trying to remove the soap suds before opening her lids. Her face feels slick, as though the soap won't rinse off.

As she opens her eyes, in the milliseconds before her mind registers that there is thick blood running down her naked body and into the drain, she realises what bothered her so much only moments ago.

She doesn't have a dog. She is still asleep.

The adrenalin rushes her body, coursing through metres of veins and arteries in an instant. She looks up at the shower to see the rich red spray shooting out, the viscous liquid slamming against her chest and bruising on impact. She screams and gropes for the dial, frantically trying to switch off the shower. Inexplicably this makes the flow stronger, pounding against her, bruising her chest, neck and face. She claws at the door, trying to slide it open, but it does not move. To her horror she realises that the blood is no longer draining away down the plughole, but is filling the cubicle. It bubbles as though being heated from below. She panics as the boiling soup reaches her ankles, then her shins, then her knees. Almost waist deep now in her prison, she slams herself against the unmoving glass, her mind flashing back to the dream of only minutes ago.

She screams for help, the sound ricocheting off the walls but drowning in the thick, waist-deep blood. The relentless flow begins to get hotter, scalding her face and upper body as her waist and legs are boiled. The stench of cooked flesh stings her nostrils, and the steam burns into her eyes. Her mind flashes to a fish in a fryer, hissing and bubbling into blisters as it cooks.

As the temperature reaches a level she can no longer bear, the revving of an engine begins to rise above the noise of the shower and her screams. The terror she feels, previously felt to be entire and at its peak, ratchets up unbearably and shudders through her body. The car smashes through the glass, momentarily reliving the pressure of the boiling water and providing a gust of cool air. As she spins toward the vehicle she knows the driver is smiling again. Above the noise of the shower, the engine, the glass smashing onto the floor, she hears his cackle. She opens her mouth to scream and wakes up again.

Two

For the second time that day, Ariadne awoke, this time in her own bed, her own house. She jerked herself up into a sitting position, studying the room for anything unusual, any tell-tale signs that might have indicated that she was still asleep.

There were none. She was awake and in the real world now.

Her duvet was half-covering her, and the only pet in her room was her cat, Harry - a fluffy black and white lump, happy only when he was sleeping or eating. True to form, he was curled up into himself on the floor, sleeping and purring contentedly. If Ariadne had made any noise while sleeping the cat clearly hadn't heard, or more likely hadn't cared.

She checked the time on her mobile phone. It was 6.20am. Her alarm was set for 6.30am so she lay back down and tried to spend ten minutes calming herself and collecting her thoughts.

After forty futile seconds of trying to erase the emotional residue of her nightmares through positive thinking - it didn't work, it never worked - she got out of bed. Opening her wardrobe, she half expected a car to race through the mirrored door, destroying the wood and shattering the glass, and then her. The furniture and trinkets in her room were no longer comforting to her, everything seemed to be tinged with the horrors of the dreams, as though the trauma of them had somehow seeped into reality, and attached themselves to the things she held dearest. Her bed was no longer a warm, inviting place. It was a harsh wasteland now, the rough blankets had been doused in acid, the once-soft pillows now carved from stone.

Every so often Harry glanced up and meowed at her, the look on his face fixed in a perpetual state of disinterest. As Ariadne left the room to go downstairs, he padded after her, purring and bouncing down the stairs alongside. They both knew who would be getting their breakfast first.

That was fine with her. Since the dreams had begun two weeks ago she never had much of an appetite.

***

The journey to work felt longer than usual. Ariadne had managed to get a seat on the train, although found herself struggling to read the newspaper through painfully tired eyes. She eventually gave up trying, and gazed out of the window at nothing for a while, not registering that she had reached her stop until the doors had closed and the train had slowly started pulling out of the platform.

She was too exhausted to react very much. She knew more than most that the best and worse things about insomnia were the dulled perceptions it afforded the recipient. Yes, it meant that silly mistakes were made – like missing a stop, or pouring juice instead of milk into a bowl of cereal – but it also meant not caring when things did go wrong. Life was experienced through a vague fog of lethargy, the myriad knocks and bumps along the way not as damaging as they could have been.

Or at least not perceived to be.

She got off at the next station and crossed the platform, managing to hop onto the next train going the opposite way. This time she didn't get a seat, and had to share what seemed to be a square inch of floor space with two businessmen and a woman holding a bunch of flowers. Ariadne didn't know the correct etiquette for holding flowers on a train, but she was pretty sure that it didn't involve flapping them into the faces of fellow commuters. Clearly, this wisdom hadn't been imparted to this woman, who seemed to think that the best way to make friends on a train was to pollinate everybody.

Ariadne held onto the last remaining millimetre of space on the greasy handrail and closed her eyes. As had been the case since the nightmares had started, she kept sensing the shadow man with the missing face. She knew he was watching, and smiling. His grin could not be seen but could be sensed, causing a ripple of fear through her soul. There was a cruelty to him, as though he were not merely a fleeting shadow, or a cloud across the sun, but an eclipse. An obstacle blocking all that is light and warm and good. He did not simply occlude the light, he destroyed it, along with any evidence that it had ever existed. As the hairs on the back of Ariadne's neck began to stand up she sprung her eyes open, bringing her back to reality.

The walk from the train station to the office took around ten minutes, although when she arrived she wouldn't have been able to remember anything notable that happened on the way. She was awake in body only, her mind still in the dream, desperately pleading with the shadow man to leave her alone, even for just one night. Long periods of sleeplessness did strange things to time, sometimes moments would stretch out for hours, other times a full day would go by seemingly in minutes. The sleep-deprived person functioned mainly on autopilot, registering and noticing nothing, but going to work, or spending time with friends, or driving long distances. All without being fully conscious of what was happening. It gave Ariadne a new appreciation for those signs on the motorway which told drivers to pull over if they felt tired.

Drivers. Cars.

Ariadne shuddered and tried to switch her focus to the present.

She got to her building and pressed the button to summon the lift. Her mind involuntarily flashed to the dream, and as the glass lift arrived she automatically thought of it filling with warm blood, the liquid rising until it forced itself into her throat, the metallic taste of life-giving blood this time taking life instead.

She steeled herself as if preparing for battle and stepped in.

When she reached her floor, she saw Anthony sitting at his desk. He was younger than her by around five years, a fact which he often liked to tease her about. They often playfully taunted each other, sometimes crossing the line into flirtation – although never anything more. He was the closest thing Ariadne had to a best friend, she was not about to complicate that with a relationship. She had other problems to sort out right now, she didn't want to add awkward fumblings and prolonged silences over the photocopier to the list.

Anthony looked up as Ariadne walked towards him. He was smiling, although the friendly grin quickly turned to concern as he saw her face.

"You dreamed about him again, didn't you?", he asked rhetorically.

Ariadne nodded.

"What was it this time, Ari? A car again, or did he find some other vehicle to run you over with?"

As Ariadne replied, she took off her coat and got settled at her desk, forcing herself to be as natural as possible.

"First he strangled me, then let go before I died. Then he drove a car into me, which pushed me out of a window at the top of a hotel. Then I woke up except I wasn't really awake, and he tried to drown me in a shower cubicle full of my own blood and then drove a car into me. It smashed the glass first and then hit me. Then I woke up properly, and here I am"

Anthony's focus sharpened as Ariadne spoke and he looked across from his monitor at her. She was typing and doing a poor job of being 'normal'.

"You had *two* dreams? That's… No wonder you look distressed. Are you alright? Maybe you should go home, Ari"

"And what would be the point in that? To fall asleep on the sofa and dream about him again? It's not occasional, it's every night. I'm being tortured and murdered *every* night"

She hadn't meant to speak so loudly but she didn't care. Tears pricked her eyes. She blinked them away and continued typing.

Anthony shook his head. He knew from personal experience how tormented a person could be by their own thoughts, and how sometimes the mind and body couldn't properly differentiate between fantasy and reality. The physiological response was the same. A panic attack is real even if the cause of it is not.

She was beginning to exhibit signs of depression, he thought. He'd spent a lot of the previous year learning about various psychological disorders and problems. He'd suffered from post-traumatic stress himself, and had found over the past few days that Ariadne seemed to be displaying some of the same symptoms.

"Ari, I'm gonna get a tea. Do you want anything?"

She nodded, understanding the shorthand they'd developed in their friendship. She got up and followed him to the small kitchen area, picking up a disposable cup from the counter and filling it with water as they spoke.

"Listen, why don't you go and see someone? I'm worried about you"

"You don't have to worry about me, Jackson, there's nothing anybody can do anyway"

She always called him by his surname – at first to tease him but now out of habit.

He took a china cup from the cupboard and flicked

the switch on the kettle.

"How do you know that?", he asked, "There are probably thousands of people who have been cured with things like this"

"Cured? I'm not ill. They're just dreams"

"Yeah but they're not though are they? You said yourself you're being tortured and mur-"

"I know what I said", she snapped, "I just don't think anybody can help. My doctor won't see me unless something's falling off, and I can't afford a psychiatrist. And I don't need one anyway. I'm not crazy, Jackson"

She registered the hurt in his eyes and immediately regretted her words.

He lightly rested his hand on her arm.

"I know you're not crazy Ari. Sometimes we can't do things on our own and need help. It doesn't make you weak. Look at me after last year. The company arranged counselling sessions for me, and these people don't usually care about anyone. Even *they* saw I needed help! I didn't want to go, but I realised I couldn't deal with things by myself. You know all this, you were there and saw it yourself, Ari! It worked for me because I tried it. All you have to do is try"

"Jackson, I appreciate what you're saying, but I can't afford a psychiatrist, and these idiots definitely aren't going to pay for a counsellor for me. Your thing happened at work, mine all happens at home"

He paused at that. She had a point.

"Tell you what, remember my friend Mina with the hypnosis and crystals and everything? She must know someone who knows about dream analysis or whatever it might be called. If she does, I'll see if you can talk to them. I was gonna ask her a few days ago actually but thought you'd get angry, but I don't think that really matters anymore Ari. This is killing you"

Ariadne flinched slightly.

"Sorry, not…killing. You know what I mean. Look, the worst that'll happen is you waste a half hour talking to someone who might be a nutcase. Although to be fair we do that on a daily basis in this place anyway"

Ariadne smiled, although her focus seemed to be somewhere else. Anthony suddenly realised that his hand was still on her arm. He whipped it away as if her skin was on fire.

Ariadne barely noticed. She absent-mindedly brought her cup to her lips and sipped some water. It was so cold she could actually feel it sliding down her pharynx, then speeding down her oesophagus into her stomach. Her mind flashed back to the shower dream and the blood in her throat, the memory triggering a rush of adrenalin. In a second her eyes refocused and she looked up at Anthony again.

"Ok. You're right. I know you're right, Jackson"

Anthony left his cup on the counter top and took out his mobile phone.

"I'll call her now. Don't worry Ari. It'll be alright"

As Ariadne took another sip of water, she wished her friend had sounded just the slightest bit convincing.

Or convinced.

Sleep No More is available in both paperback and ebook formats.

For more information go to
www.angelomarcos.com